MEN OF MASABA

ALSO BY HUMPHREY HARMAN

Tales Told near a Crocodile
African Samson

The Viking Press New York

Men of Masaba

Humphrey Harman

This book is for Stella Bwisa,
a daughter of the Bukusu who
talked well about her people.

Map by Laurel Brown

First Edition

First published in 1971 by The Viking Press, Inc.
625 Madison Avenue, New York, N.Y. 10022
Published simultaneously in Canada by
The Macmillan Company of Canada Limited
Library of Congress catalog card number: 73-150117
Fic 1. Folklore and Legend—Africa

Printed in U.S.A.
Trade 670-46892-4 VLB 670-46893-2

1 2 3 4 5 75 74 73 72 71

CONTENTS

Chikhu chisala likokhe
"From wood one gets ashes."
Bukusu proverb

AUTHOR'S NOTE

A people called the Bukusu live in western Kenya, and if no one outside of East Africa, except for a few specialists, has ever heard of them, then that is no more than can be expected. They are a small tribe, only one out of the hundreds in Africa. Their land is fertile, they are skillful farmers, and they have a salty sense of humor and a streak of willful independence. Their neighbors call them stubborn. They differ little from many other minor African tribes.

They live within a triangle formed by three great features of this geographically exuberant part of the continent: Lake Victoria, an inland water whose size beggars belief; the Rift Valley, that ancient but still disturbing catastrophe to the earth's surface which runs from Palestine to Southern Africa; and Mount Elgon.

Elgon is the smallest of East Africa's three great volcanic peaks, but it is far from being negligible. A scant fifty miles from the equator, it still shows snow upon its 14,000-foot crater wall during cool weather. In the rain forests that bury its vast slopes you can find many of Africa's animals, from the elephant to the rare, shy pangolin. There is even supposed to be a mythical beast, the Nandi Bear. The Bukusu call the mountain Masaba, and, if their accounts are to be believed, they have lived on or near it for a very long time.

Like most Africans south of the Sahara, they were until recent times illiterate. But again, like most African peoples, they can give an oral account of their past. It is not history as we know it—the kind that is being revealed in learned papers from brand-new universities all over the continent. Bukusu "history" as told by the unlearned is a succulent brew of myths, legends of the George Washington's-cherry-tree genre, records of possible validity, fables, jokes, and cautionary tales. And all in little discernable order. Quite reasonably so; in what order could such disparate material be placed?

This tale is "history" of that sort. Much of its skeleton was given to me by Bukusu, or by men and women from neighboring tribes. Sometimes I have romanced, but it should not be assumed that because an incident seems far-fetched it was necessarily invented by me. For instance, I have some authority for citing so extraordinary a method of choosing a chief as the pouring of milk down a hillside.

I am not conscious of plagiarism. Something like Kokanya's ribald kilt-lifting in answer to his men's concern for their wives and children occurs in Herodotus; but I heard the incident described by a Nandi who certainly had never read the *History*. The same man also gave me the Boccaccio-like story of Merikwa's two wives as a legend of his people, and here I have corroboration. The anthropologist Peristiany also heard it, for in a study of the Kipsigis, a closely related tribe, he records the tale in both vernacular and literal translations.

But it is true that often I have invented, and I am cheerfully unrepentant about this. There is no doubt that a great number of Bukusu, long dead, did the same thing before I laid hands upon their story.

H.H.

Chalimbana, 1970

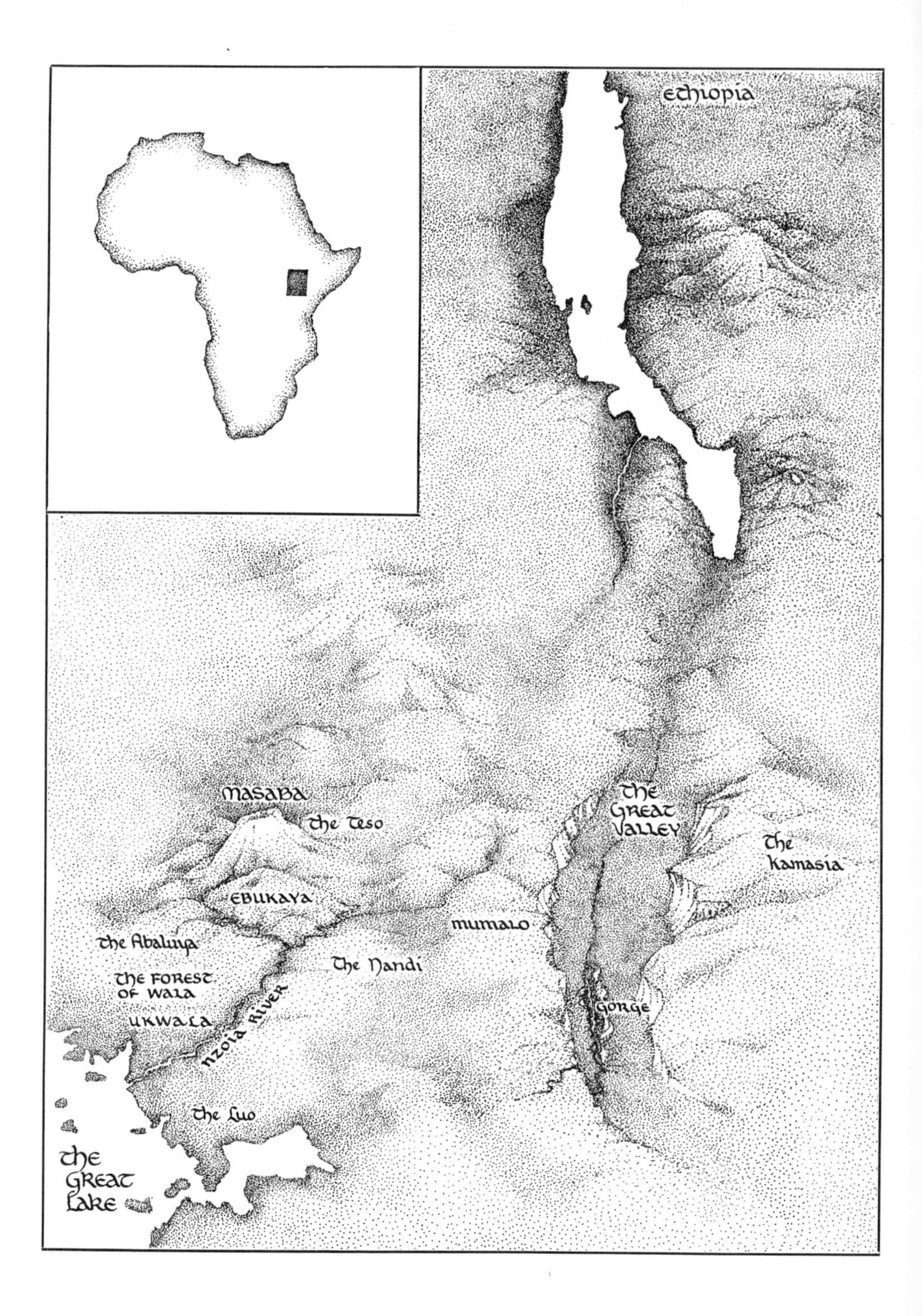
Ethiopia
Masaba
The Teso
The Great Valley
The Kamasia
Ebukaya
Mumalo
The Abaluya
The Nandi
The Forest of Wala
Gorge
Ukwala
Nzoia River
The Luo
The Great Lake

Libina

The story of the Bukusu people begins with a man called Libina. But before Libina is dealt with, something must be said of what came earlier, if only that Libina may be credible as a man. For of this one, unlike other names which for a brief moment break out of the darkness behind him, it can be said that he was as we are. Libina did not come from the clouds that cover the great mountain Masaba or the cavern that cradled the snake Eyabebe, or any similar mysterious place. He was a man and came from seed and a woman. But as the egg in the nest is not the beginning but the bird before it, and yet not that either, and so on back to who knows what parentless hatching, so it is for Libina and the Bukusu. If his story and theirs is not to be plucked from nothing and no cause, like maggots breeding in meat, then what came before him must be touched upon.

It is said—one cannot be more definite—that the wanderings of the Bukusu began in Ethiopia, where other, bigger tribes came from. When it began and why are unknown. What is certain is that at some time they touched Mbayi in the Great Valley and stayed there long enough to mark stones that can still be read today by those skilled enough to do so. Leaving Mbayi, they circled Masaba to the north—but slowly, slowly. Each bite of distance covered on the journey was a matter of burning land clean, of sowing and reaping millet for their beer, of the decay of poor thatched houses, of birth and death. And they increased, for by the time Uganda was reached they were numerous enough to be called a small people, the Bukusu.

At Tororo they lived side by side with the Masai, which, although it may sound strange today, was possible then because the Masai were small and unimportant and had not yet grown the vulture's appetite to prey on all men that came later. Certainly the two peoples lived, and afterward moved, together and in peace, though jostling and hooking to their flanks like migrating buck. Also the Bukusu caught something of the Masai way of life, and their food was milk and meat and blood with a little millet grown for beer. The last place they knew going north was Mwali in Malakisi, and here we come to the man Libina and firmer ground.

Now there are several ways of telling Libina's story and none of them agrees in every particular. So there must be a choice, and the one displayed here is the best. And did someone ask, "Also the truest?"

Well, this is something difficult to answer. Who is to know the truth about what happened so long ago that the time since cannot easily be counted in seasons or even in lifetimes? What is to be said?

That in a way it is true? That it is partly true? That it is true as the spider knows truth when she creeps into the house and listens to the words spoken and watches what is done? She cannot get exactly right all that is heard and seen because she does not understand.

It is as true as the mouth that tells it and the ear that listens.

It was at Mwali that the Bukusu were tormented by the snake Eyabebe.

They lived in the shadow of Masaba. Shaggy with forests, cloud-misted, filling the world to the west, it sheltered them, a presence felt even when unseen because of the storms and rain it bred. The slopes marched down from the distant crater—cradle of gods and spirits, bald and blue, remote as death. Below the forests, the slopes plunged to the plain in great cliffs of pitted red stone, and from the lips of these the rivers sprang in splendid curving falls and their rainbows played in the sun. Even when the leaves hung limp on the plain and the cattle panted in the heat, these waters numbed the scooping hand.

The cliff ran almost unbroken, but midway along its length there was a narrow crack in the rock, shaped like a woman's part and hung with ferns and creepers, and in this the creature lived. Behind its entrance the cave must have widened into vast halls, for when Eyabebe was hungry it bellowed like the great male goat Elayo, and men could hear the echoes retreating deep within the cliff. But how far the caves reached only the snake knew. It fed about once a month, coil after coil emerging from the rock to devastate the land, and it was so insatiable that cattle and sheep went in scores down its maw before it was satisfied.

The people did not lack courage, only means. At first, time after time the young men gathered at the cave mouth but when it came out, coldly ravening, they could not withstand it. The great body would wrap a man in its embrace and the rest fled, hearing behind them a rib cage cracking in the tightening grasp.

For years this was a land troubled by Eyabebe. Men moved their herds and homes far from the deep grass at the cliff's edge, grazing cattle there only when the snake was quiet. But for much of the time the good black soil that held the rain, the sweet rivers, and the tall grass were wasted. They made do with starved land to the north and mourned a wealth which was in their sight but not their grasp. Indeed, the snake spoiled all.

Libina was born to the Masai clans and when he came to manhood he was cut, for at this time the Masai circumcised their youth as they do today, though the Bukusu did not yet have the custom. So when Libina had heard the secrets and learned the precepts he waited his turn in the moonlight with an uncle standing to either side, and watched boy after boy before him walk stiffly from the ordeal while the crowd murmured approval at their courage. Presently he too stood before the laibon, and maybe the moonlight showed black patches on the trampled earth at his feet and perhaps he was slow to grasp what they were. However it was, the boy did a strange thing for one who was to become such a man, for when the elder's dry hand was on him and the pain slashed red through his loins, he winced and twisted and mewed through clenched teeth. And doubtless he heard his uncles hiss.

When the boys are cut they take their pain and pride away from people into some lonely place and stay there until they are healed, but usually they go in twos or threes to comfort each other with boasting. Since Libina had done the unforgivable thing, he took for company only a failure that would stay with him and his clan for a lifetime. He went to a small hillock on the plain, covered with thorn trees, and there he must have pondered the unfairness of his misery and the pains of second birth and unhealed wound. And when these things grew numb, as with time they do, he found that through the scattered thorns he had a view of the snake's door. All was quiet there, for the beast had fed with the full moon and this was long past now. So, for lack of occupation, he thought of the snake and, since there was time, his mind stabbed deep into the problem of Eyabebe.

His eye measured the narrowness of the crack, beginning low down near the grass, and there the palm of a hand held flat would have bridged it. Then it opened, its widest part coming just below where a man could reach, and after this it shrank again to a slit which vanished behind the ferns clinging to the rock.

"Now," reasoned Libina, "it's said that the snake is as broad as the chest of an ox. If that is so there is perhaps only half of one spear's length of this doorway he can use to go in and out. Hmm! And that just within the reach of a man standing below."

By now the idea that came to him had driven away the nagging of both wound and shame.

"But it would be best if I had a little help in this matter," said Libina.

Since he knew there was nothing to be gained from his

own people, he went to the young men of a Bukusu clan which lived nearby and said, "Come with me when the moon is full, for I've a plan that might rid us of Eyabebe."

The young men stared at him and considered, and then one of them spat and said, "If you go below the cave and search in the grass, no doubt you'll find some of the droppings of the snake. Choose a dry turd and prize it open with your spear and perhaps you'll see the bones of men who spoke like you. But look closely, for they'll be ground very small. Go home, Cut One, and when you're healed find something more worthwhile to occupy you."

"It was only a suggestion," replied Libina, "but when the full moon has gone don't forget that I offered a Bukusu a name."

Then he returned to the hill and polished his plan.

Presently he found two full-grown cork trees which were in red flower but not yet leafed, and he felled them both with his simi and shaped the trunks like the upper and lower halves of the cleft rock of Eyabebe. He took three days over it for although their wood was soft, they were large and he was alone. When the trees were trimmed to his satisfaction he brought them one by one to the cave mouth. Asis must have helped him, for he was barely a man and still weak from the privations of his ordeal. When he had the timbers at the cave mouth, he compared them again with the slant of the rock, trimmed a little further, and then thrust one upward into the vault and the other downward so that the narrowing rock bit into the cork and held like clenched teeth.

Eh! The ghosts of the dead must have helped him, for otherwise no man could have done it.

During all this time Eyabebe did not stir. The snake must

have been deep in the caverns asleep and heard nothing.

"Now," said Libina, "there's only one place where this devil can try to come out and that's narrower than the chest of an ox, so we won't see all of him. Unless, of course, the wood gives, and if that happens there'll be a few more bones in the droppings among the grass, and I don't know that I care much which way it goes."

Then he sat down to wait, and to pass the time he took a piece of pumice and honed his simi until it was as sharp as his resolve.

He waited six days and lived on the hyrax he killed, for they were plentiful there on the lower ledges of the cliff, and he had no fear of the snake's coming by day. In the afternoons he slept and at evening drank from a nearby stream, but at night he waited below the cave and ran a thumb over the edge of the simi and watched.

On the seventh night, when the moon was full, he heard the cave stir, and, deep inside, the thing bellowed like Elayo the male goat. He counted each roar repeated seven times before it died to a whisper in the folds of the rock. Then he stood to one side of the cave entrance, pressed against the cliff, and gathered his strength.

He did not have long to wait. Soon the snake thrust out its head and a length of neck and the soft wood wedged the bulk that followed and held. And while it bawled, Libina whirled back the simi and cut.

One cut he made. Just one, and the head fell bounding among the grasses while the man almost drowned in cold green blood. For seven days that lopped neck bled, and where the slime soaked into the ground the grass withered and never grew again.

But Libina did not wait to see the end of this. He went

back to the Bukusu village, bent and staggering beneath the burden of the head, flung it down among the young men, and said, "I have killed Eyabebe."

This was how Libina became the first war chief of both tribes. All the clan leaders, both Masai and Bukusu, swore he should be obeyed in war and in such matters as touched the well-being of both peoples. In other affairs, of course, each held to its own customs and council.

Little else is known about him—how long he lived, the names and number of his children, and the small things that shape a man in the minds of those who come after him. Of these there is no memory, but one other story is told of Libina; it is this.

When he was dying, he asked the elders of all the clans to come to him and said, "You made me your war chief and swore I should be obeyed. Now there is one last thing I would tell you to do, and since it touches custom rather than those matters where I was given authority, I must beg and not command. If we are to be recognized as one people and hold together, a sign must be laid upon every man and woman."

Those who were listening agreed.

"Then," continued Libina, "to my mind the sign should be this. When any man among us is full grown, able to bear arms and kill, of an age to put seed into a woman, ripe enough to know the secrets of his sex and people, then he should be circumcised. Women also, when the signs of maturity are found on them, when they are able to till the ground and prepare food, open to receive a man's seed and bring out the new people sleeping within, they should be circumcised."

Now when the elders had considered, they agreed that this should be done. Perhaps, faced with the dying Libina and overawed, the matter was not studied so long as it might have been, for certainly because of their agreement trouble came later. However it was, when Libina died both tribes began circumcising men and women and that is how the custom came to the Bukusu. But in other ways they became less of one people, for the Masai chose one chieftain and the Bukusu another, though who these men were is unknown. Still the peoples remained together, two oxen yoked.

Libina plucks the people out of the darkness for a moment, then it closes again. Now comes a time when we can see figures moving, catch the dull glint of spears; women trudging laden with household goods, herded cattle vague in enveloping dust. This is how it must have been, for they were wandering again, but no single face is plain.

Later they were at a place named Sirikwa, though where that was remains a mystery, for the name is unknown today. However, in this place the unwise haste shown by the elders at Libina's death ripened to harvest. Trouble rose between Masai and Bukusu and it came in this way.

The Masai had obeyed Libina and circumcised both men and women; the Bukusu did not. Their men came of age and stood before the laibons and were cut, but the women refused. They declared that it took away the pleasure to be got from men. The malicious said they were afraid.

Now because of this the Masai men would have nothing to do with Bukusu women. They called them filthy creatures and would only lie with or marry women of their own tribe. The Bukusu girls were offended and tattled to their young men, who took their part, and this led to war between the tribes. We do not know whether it was a great battle or a long-winded bickering, but whichever it was, the Masai were the stronger and drove the Bukusu away from Sirikwa.

The tribes separated and never joined again.

Maina

Maina was born at Sirikwa to the Masaba clan, though we do not know the names of his parents. Too young to take any part in the fighting between Masai and Bukusu, he came to manhood during the long retreat to Mumalo, which is where the Bukusu clans went first. There on the high, grass-covered plains above the Great Valley, they decided to settle, since at that time the land was empty. There were six clans, all weary and depleted of fighting men from their war with the Masai, and it is worthwhile saying a little about them.

Three were Bukusu proper—the Omufuini, Omubichachi, and Omwahala—and these did not intermarry since such an act might have brought confusion of blood. Instead their men looked for wives from the other clans, when they did not go outside the tribe for women.

The three remaining clans were the Masaba, the Babukusu, and the Chetung'eng'i. The Masaba were a mixture of many tribes, originally tenants of the Bukusu who had gathered themselves together under a leader of that name and had, by their spears, earned the right to a say in the tribe's affairs. It is possible that this man had taken his name from the mountain. The Babukusu were a hiving off from the Teso people, a group too weak to stand alone during the wars of the past, who had been granted clanship among the Bukusu. The Chetung'eng'i, as can be guessed from the sound of their name, were of Masai blood and custom and we do not know why they did not side with their own people at Sirikwa. They were famous for their laibons, who presided at circumcisions, doctored both cattle and men, and dealt in magic. The laibons were respected and feared by all the Bukusu, and the warriors also were as formidable as wounded buffalo. Indeed, "Chetung'eng'i" means Buffalo Men.

During the stay at Sirikwa there had been changes of custom. Curdled milk and blood was still eaten, and cattle remained the main wealth and pride. But now they kept sheep and goats as well, for meat. Also they grew finger millet and made porridge as well as beer with it. They carried the seed of this with them to Mumalo, and everyone made haste to break land and plant even before they built huts, for the long rains were upon them and they were desperate for a crop. The cold rains of Mumalo made it a bad place to lie in rough shelters, and the old people and the children coughed, many dying from lung sickness. That is how Mumalo gained the name of the Land of Coughing.

When the crop was safely sown, they turned to house-building to escape from the hail and cold nights, but when the houses had been up for some time many of them took fire and burned to the ground. The fires always began secretly in the thatch, smoldering deep within and then suddenly taking hold, and families choked and died in their sleep. Some explained this by the grass being wet and green when it was used for thatching, but others looked wider and asserted that the spirits of the place were against them. And it is true that they had taken possession in unwise haste, making no trial of the land's disposition first. This matter of burned houses caused a great deal of fearful muttering, but later that year a woman of the Omufuini was found in witchcraft by the laibons and her guilt proved. When she had been hacked to death, the fires stopped and the people took heart.

Now that they had done what they could to secure the future in material matters, there was time to deal with the ceremonial side of life. For nearly three years no boy or girl had been initiated into maturity, for, during the wars with the Masai and the wandering, there had been neither leisure nor scope to do this. And so there were youths with broad shoulders and women with heavy breasts who chafed and muttered under the name of children. It was beginning to show in flaring tempers, quick blows, and babies born for whom no ancestor could be named to inhabit, who of necessity must be hurried away, strangled, and forgotten by everyone but the girl who had pleasured and suffered for them. The people now made haste to put this right. The women took the girls aside and instructed them in their own mysteries, and the boys were made men in a great ceremony which lasted for three entire nights. It is said that the laibon was old and his hand trembled and because of this the youths suffered more than is usual.

Maina was made a man then, and since there is no record of how he behaved, it is safe to believe that he stood without flinching and earned the approval of all who were there to judge his courage. But then Maina was not the kind of man to have earned a bad name by shrinking from a little pain.

We also know he was of unusual height and strength and had waited long for circumcision.

When the young men were healed, they were equipped by their families with spears and shields and banded together in groups. They were age brothers, a relationship that cut across clan so that Omufuini might find himself brigaded with Masaba or Chetung'eng'i. The youths were given a stiffening of older warriors to lead them and dispatched north to hunt and scout. This was done to educate and harden them and also to provide occupation. The elders wanted no young bulls bursting with mischief idling in the villages.

Mumalo plain stops suddenly to the east where the near slope of the Great Valley begins. The wall here is high and steep, descending in great broken steps, and the valley beneath, wide and divided by a river. This runs strongly during the rains and also when flash storms occur to the north. Then the banks are buried in flood water and the river is difficult to cross. In the dry season it shrinks to a string of yellow pools or retreats to the bottom of echoing gorges, and the valley, penned between its walls in the heat, becomes a place where only a snake would wish to live. The far-valley slopes, a good day's march away, are also steep but, unlike Mumalo, crowned with great forests. At that time these were empty except for small bands of

Dorobo, a people most skilled at hunting and hiding. Usually all one sees of Dorobo are hollow trees still smoldering where the bees have been smoked out and robbed of honey.

But to concern ourselves with those men who went north, Maina among them.

North from Mumalo plain, the land falls gently until it joins and becomes one floor with the Great Valley. Here there is no distinguishing feature until the mountains of Ethiopia are reached. It is true that there are families of rocky hills which seem important to a traveler grown accustomed to nothing more striking than an ant heap, as a well-worn wife looks good enough when one has traveled far from the beauty of a neighbor's daughter. The country grows hot and dry, the rivers are small, for most of the year empty of all but smooth sand and whitened rocks. After the rains the grass grows yellow and dry and is broken by fierce winds from the west, and the leafless thorn branches rattle like seeds in a dried gourd.

But the sixty or so young men marching north found grass still with sap in it and water in the rivers. The leather war bags they carried were no burden, for their people had had little grain to spare; the harvest would not come for a month. So the half-cooked millet meal, dampened and pounded hard, came but a little way up each man's bag. This troubled them not at all, for farther north game was seen in such numbers as the oldest man among them had never known before. Hartebeeste, zebra, wildebeeste, and other antelope swarmed in herds thick as locusts, all patiently moving north, keeping pace with the men. And aloof from these were great armies of buffalo, heavy, suspicious, and dangerous. The Bukusu left the buffalo alone but they fell upon the flanks of the other herds and killed almost as they wished, and it was strange to see a speared buck lie kicking in death throes while those near it scarcely lifted their heads from grazing. They were like men drugged with the smoke of hemp leaves.

So all ate fresh meat until the last crammed gobbet refused to go down their throats, but they were provident enough to sun-dry as much again and fill the bags. It did not seem to them that such plenty could last.

Lions also were busy at the same task as the men. They saw great prides by day and built fires against them at night. But there was enough meat for both and to spare, and no necessity to vex each other.

After some days the game thinned, the herds turning east, and the men went on alone. And soon after this they saw smoke in the distance, not the rolling clouds of a bush fire, but the faint slanting lines that come from cooking fires fed with dry thorn and a little ant mud mixed with the kindling. They halted and discussed what to do, and the upshot was that Bokoli, who was their leader, sent five men forward to find out what they had to deal with. They were instructed to go secretly, using their eyes and ears rather than their spears. This Bokoli was a man of middle age who had done well enough in the past, but his reputation was for steady counsel rather than fighting ability. It was possibly for this reason that the elders had made him leader of these largely untried men. No one had ever found fault with Bokoli's courage; it was only that he was prudent.

Among the five who went forward was Maina. There was a small hill to the left of them that seemed as if it might overlook the fires, and so they made for this, keeping in the cover of a dried watercourse. They reached the hill, unseen so far as they knew, and from the rocks at the top there was a good view.

Below and curving away to either side were many small groups of shelters made from brush and skins, and by each of these villages were large cattle kraals roughly built of thorn boughs. They were empty but within them the dung was piled high, dark-colored and fresh. Women and children were outside the houses, but not many. The women were dressed in cowskins from which the hair had been scraped, and their upper arms were hidden with ranked bracelets that caught the sun. Some warriors were there also, lean, slight men, and the spears they carried had long blades fishtailed at the shaft end like the leaves of a cocoyam. In every direction across the plain great herds of cattle grazed, and with them were many armed herdsmen. These were a numerous people, for the five who watched from the top of the hill could see no end to the shelters and the herds and, beyond, smoke dribbled up from yet more fires.

It was the first sight the Bukusu had of the Kamasia people, and the five went back to Bokoli and soberly reported what they had seen.

After he had listened, Bokoli told them they had done well. "It's plain," he said, "that these are a great people, and since the houses they build are only shelters for a few days, they must be a people in movement. Also there isn't grass enough here to support herds of the size you describe for long. They are moving and it's possible they may come south to Mumalo. We must return and give warning."

But Maina thought otherwise.

"Before we go," he said, "let's try to take some of those cattle. They were good beasts to my eye, and I'd like to see some of them in a kraal of my own."

"That wouldn't be wise," replied Bokoli. "We can't do much against so many. If we did manage to gather some beasts we could only move slowly with them. These people are numerous enough to detach many men to follow. *They* won't travel at the pace of a cow and will be too many to fight. If we cling to the cattle we'll get the worst of it, and if we leave them and run, what is gained?"

"I still think we'd be small men if it wasn't tried," said Maina.

"I thought that I was war leader here," said Bokoli, who did not like this talk of small men. "I was using a spear before anyone ever thought of trusting you with one. Now let's put an end to this talk and go home."

"You'll have to put up with the talk a little longer yet," said Maina, wagging a forefinger. "It's true that you've a certain reputation. But as I remember, it is that of a man who says, 'Better not put your hand near the bee hole or you'll get stung,' rather than one who does substantial work with a spear. Also to me you sound like someone who's already got a good store of beasts in his kraal and is prepared to let them increase by nature. At present I'm not in that fortunate position but I wouldn't mind being so. I think this might be the time when it could turn out that way."

This appealed to the others there, for what Maina said about cattle also touched most of them, and when Bokoli tried to speak again he was shouted down. When he saw that he was not going to be followed, he said, "If you are going to do this, then I can no longer lead, for my counsel is against it. Someone else must command, Maina or another; that you must decide. But understand this: whoever it is, I'll follow and perhaps we'll see if my spear work is as poor as Maina thinks it is."

Then he sat down and would take no further part in what was said, but only asked them to let him know when they were to move and what he was to do.

They made Maina leader and the plan he made was this.

From the hill he had noticed that one group of shelters with its kraal was set a little apart from the rest. The kraal was large and the dung in it plentiful so it seemed that at night it must house a large herd. They would go to the hill so that the place they had to work in could be seen by all and wait there until dark, and while they waited they would divide into two groups, a large and a small. At dark the larger group would move down near the kraal and wait, while the smaller one would circle the village and attack it from the other side with a great deal of noise. They would burn a shelter or two and do everything possible to draw attention, but before the fighting became serious they would slip away.

Those by the kraal would hold off until the guards were drawn away to the attack upon the village. Then they would rush the kraal, kill anyone remaining, take what cattle they could manage, and begin herding them homeward. Meanwhile those who had attacked the village would follow and deal with anyone who came after them.

It was not a new plan, but it was one that had often done well in the past. When Bokoli heard it—for in spite of all he had said he could not restrain himself from listening, as a man usually does when his fate is being discussed—he said, "Khakaba help us, we're dead men."

It went much as Maina had planned. He led the smaller group and they killed a number of Kamasia without great bother, for the men were muddled with sleep and preoccupied with the safety of their women and children. The houses were fired and made a fine blaze, and it was not until the guards came running from the kraal that the fight grew hot. The Bukusu lost a couple of men before they broke off and retreated into the dark. Perhaps they should have left sooner than they did, but Maina was anxious that those at the kraal make a worthwhile haul, and held his men until he reckoned there had been time for this. Once whistled off, they circled the burning houses and started in the direction that had been decided. The Kamasia followed at first, but not seriously, for by now they had discovered the rifled kraal and were uncertain how big the raiding party was. After clashing with Maina once more in the dark and losing a man, they decided to go back, get help from neighbors, and wait for daylight when they could see more clearly how large the problem was.

So by dawn Maina had caught up with the drovers and put a good distance between himself and the Kamasia. He had gained a large herd and done it at the slight cost of three men. It appeared to him that things had gone well and he said so to Bokoli, who had been with those at the village and who, it must be admitted, had done good work.

"The part of the scorpion that hurts is at the other end," said Bokoli. "What are you going to do when a good half of that tribe comes looking for their cows?"

"I had thought of postponing that meeting for a while,"

replied Maina, and then he did the second thing that was to give him the beginning of a name.

On their journey north they had encountered and avoided a place where the plain lost all soil and became bare rock littered with loose pumice. It was perhaps an hour's travel across and very uncomfortable to walk upon. It lay half a day's march south, and when they reached it Maina halted the herd and took from it all the unthrifty-looking creatures, the young bulls and cows with calves. These he put in the charge of five men. He told them to herd east for the rest of the day, and to mill the cattle about as they did so to make the spoor appear to come from more beasts than there were. When night came they must abandon them and rejoin the main party at a big river course ahead. Maina watched the five drive their beasts east and then started the rest across the pumice where they would leave little trace behind them. To make sure, he directed twenty men to walk behind the herd scraping up any dung dropped and putting it into war bags. There was little enough to bother with because it had been a long time since the beasts had grazed, but Maina wanted to make sure. "Did you collect dung with Maina?" came to be a question that men later asked of boasters who wearied them and needed to be put down.

After crossing the pumice and pushing on farther for some hours, they halted, for the cattle were desperate to graze and the men's feet sore from the hot rock. That evening in the cool time they went on for two hours more to the river. There was still enough water standing for the cattle and men, and they slept the remainder of the night while the cattle grazed again.

At dawn the five who had left the day before came in and reported that the trick had succeeded, for after abandoning the herd they had laid up for the rest of the day in a hidden place. Toward evening the Kamasia had arrived, a war band twice the size of the Bukusu. They had dispatched a handful of men back with the recovered cattle, and then done a certain amount of casting about to discover what had become of the rest before it became too dark to see tracks. The five had then left their hiding place and walked most of the night.

"So it appears we've gained a day at least before they discover our direction," said Maina. "And I think just one more day after that before they get sight of us."

"Delay won't improve their tempers," said Bokoli.

"We'll find occupation for them when they come," said Maina. "And while we're discussing this, I'd like to make it clear that you're beginning to weary me. Pushing a spear through you might save a great deal of tiresome conversation."

"You'd best save the spear-pushing until the day after tomorrow," replied Bokoli. "It would be a pity to waste on me now something you might need in another direction then."

The next day they traveled again, more slowly now because the cattle were tiring. Maina left a small party of men two hours' march behind them to watch for the Kamasia, and it was noticed that all day he measured the country they passed through with a speculative eye. The Bukusu were no longer as carefree as they had been, for it seemed to many of them that although they had done well so far, things might yet end badly.

Toward evening they reached a point where the land begins to slope up to Mumalo. It was a slow ascent and there was as yet many days' march before they would see the Bukusu huts, for the way rises in broad steps, scattered with great rocks and thickets of creeping thorn and candelabra. Here the baobab of the lower country grows stunted and vanishes. The Great Valley now lay to the left, and cutting across their path were occasional broad, steep-sided gulleys where old rivers had once run into it.

That evening, on the edge of one of these, Maina stopped and considered and then walked back, thoughtfully looking to left and right. When he had seen what he wanted, the cattle went past him down into the gulley and halted for the night. The place was roomy and although no water was visible in the river course, elephant had been digging in the sand, and by doing the same the men uncovered enough water to satisfy both themselves and the cattle. The hidden stream had kept the grass living on both banks, and the animals fell on this hungrily while the Bukusu ate dried meat, rested, and waited for the scouts to catch up. When they came they reported no sign yet of the Kamasia, and after he had listened, Maina let them eat and drink before sending them back along the way they had come, with orders to find a good place, lie up, and watch. They were to stay there until they saw the pursuit, then leave without being detected and return quickly to the valley. Maina put guards above the bluff on the dangerous side of the gulley and that night everyone else slept his fill and was grateful for it, for sleep was something they had gone somewhat short of since the fight at the kraal.

The next morning Maina gathered everyone about him

and described what he proposed to do. They heard him out and it is said that afterward they were silent and Maina was uncertain whether they would follow him. Most of them were raw warriors whom the past few weeks had sorely tried, and the report of the numbers of the Kamasia to be dealt with had made them over-thoughtful. Then Bokoli spoke up and said this:

"Our Bukusu way is for all to have a say in who should lead us in war. And when every man who wants to speak has done so, then the opinion of the most is followed, and whoever they name is leader. Now, there is another side to our custom and it is this. When the war leader has been named, the time for talk is over, and we who follow do so as long as the man's luck stays with him. It doesn't appear to me that Maina's luck has taken wings yet. It was there when we took the cattle and again when we fooled their owners two days back. Therefore it would seem to me sensible to do as he tells us a third time. If we fail, then that's another matter and we might have to think further about the wisdom of our choice."

When he had finished they agreed to fight in the way Maina wished them to, and that was an end to their doubts.

"I'm inclined to be glad now that I didn't drive that spear through you as I thought of doing," said Maina to Bokoli afterward.

And so, the talking finished, Maina led the Bukusu back to the top of the bluff and told every man where to go and what to do when the testing time came. That done three or four times to make it go home and stick, they returned to the bottom and passed the day pleasantly enough except for a nagging anxiety about the future. They ground their spears sharp on pumice stones and repaired such shields as required it, and the hardier spirits among them slept in the shade near the grazing herd. In the early evening, the scouts appeared above and shouted that the Kamasia were coming. Everyone took weapons and climbed to his place. They hid behind rocks and in thickets for a hundred paces beyond the gulley's edge, well to the right and left of the cattle trail leading below. The beasts stayed where they were in plain sight of any man above. They were beginning to bunch together, as they do at evening, and would not shift far. It was remarked afterward that during all this, not a word was spoken except to the scouts, who had to be led to the hiding places arranged for them.

Then they waited, but not for long. Presently the Kamasia came, loping like a pack of starved wild dogs. They were formidable men, running easily, faces painted with red mud peering from circlets of black-and-white colobus fur. Red-and-white cowhide shields were slung on their backs, the taut skins making hollow drum noises as they bumped. They were strung out like maize grains leaking from a bag, and as the leaders ran between the hidden Bukusu to the gulley's edge Maina noted the sweat darkening the dusty flesh and their dry panting mouths. Running all day in the heat across the low country and now up the long slope, these men would be thirsty and tired.

The leaders halted at the rim and looked down. Seeing the cattle below, they raised a shout. Two thirds of them were bunched between the jaws of the trap, babbling like hornbills, when Maina signaled to a man crouched behind him. A cow horn blared harshly and the Bukusu rose in concert, bounded three or four paces, and stabbed.

Half the red men died where they stood, before they could lift spear or unsling shield. Those lining the gulley edge went down the steep pumice slope either dead or alive, most of them dead for they could be seen lying broken and still at the bottom. The rest fled down the stream bank and took no further part. Only those lagging behind, with time to see what was happening, made any account of themselves. This remainder gathered into some kind of fighting formation and were ready when Maina collected his men. Then the Kamasia showed quality enough, but they were far from happily placed. On the wrong side of the slope, the charge against them had weight and speed and doubtless the slaughter they had witnessed had not raised their hearts. But for a time they fought like leopards. Then they broke and fled back into the haze of the plain from which they had come. The Bukusu let them go and busied themselves finishing off any wounded who remained and reckoning their own dead.

And this was how it turned out at the battle the Bukusu call Maina's Battle. It went far in setting him on his journey to become war leader of his people. It cost some twenty men dead and a few more who died later from wounds. Among these was Bokoli, and Maina was heard to say that he was sorry it had turned out that way.

Maina did not immediately become war leader of the Bukusu; he was too young for his betters to stomach that. But he had gained a great name and he led the young warriors of his age group, for they would follow no other man. Also, with a leader's share of the cattle taken from the Kamasia, he was now something of a man of substance and he soon married for the first time, a girl from the Babukusu. But there will be more said later about Maina's dealings with women.

The main concern of everyone after his return with the cattle was the threat of the Kamasia coming south. Obviously they were a great cattle people; the good grasslands of Mumalo lay in their path and it was likely that they would regard them with a covetous eye. The times promised trouble, and if it came to fighting, the Bukusu were not at all sure that they would come off best. The war leader, a man from the Omufuini named Miendo, dispatched a group of scouts north to keep an eye on Kamasia movements, and most of the Bukusu cattle were moved to grazing grounds south of Mumalo where they would be safer from raids.

When the news came it convinced the elders that they had good reason to be concerned. The scouts sent word that the whole tribe came steadily south, moving their shelters every day or so. Also, small parties of Kamasia warriors were sighted spying out the land near Mumalo. There was much troubled discussion among the Bukusu and many were against staying to see what fighting would decide. The harvest was in, and while it had not been a great one, still there was enough food to tide the people over a move without too much hunger.

While this uncertainty was at its height, some of the scouts returned with a tale that seemed to settle the matter. Without a doubt the Kamasia were moving to take Mumalo. They had left behind their women and children and a few boys and old men to hold the cattle together, and all the fighting men were marching south in full war gear. They did not seem to have any doubts about dealing with the Bukusu, as they were moving without any attempt at secrecy, and here, said the scouts, they probably had the right of it, for there were many more fighting men than the Bukusu could field.

When this was known, those who clamored to leave seemed to have hold of the right end of the spear. The clan leaders, elders, and important warriors whom Miendo called together for a great meeting believed that how and where they should move was the matter to be discussed. But at this council, Maina put forward a plan which, after it had been looked at narrowly, seemed to have some chance of success. After a great deal of bitter argument they agreed to try what he proposed.

And so the Bukusu did this. They called every man who could fight into one army. Then they hastily assembled all the women and armed them with old spears and broken shields and, when the store of these gave out, with long sticks and flat winnowing baskets. They collected every hide they could find which would serve as a kilt or body skin and made the women wear these, and some of them fabricated rough headgear of feathers and oxtails. Then both men and women marched north to a place that seemed to suit the plan. It was where the long swell of land breasting up to the plain leveled out. There was a shallow pass here, a wide grassy place with low hills to the back of it. Across the pass they put their warriors in close ranks, making the most of their numbers. To either side of the pass and not too well hidden, were armed boys with a few men. And at a distance, on the inner slopes of the hills behind, were all the women. They sat wrapped in their cloaks, rank upon rank, with spears and sticks held upright between their knees, and their backs turned to where the enemy was expected so that even a keen eye would not see that these warriors had breasts.

So when the Kamasia appeared out of the dead ground of the rise they saw before them a great army. There was a chest of picked men to slow and blunt their first charge, a hint of horns at the flanks to gore them when they were occupied with the chest, and behind, confident in their great numbers, but faced away from the battle so that excitement would not draw them in prematurely, the main body of the Bukusu army.

The Kamasia halted, and doubtless the leaders discussed what lay before them and spoke bitterly of the incompetence of their spies. Then they returned without putting things to the test. The tribe shifted its line of march east, first into the Great Valley and then up its far side to the forested hills of Baringo. There they settled and were in the future of little trouble to the Bukusu except for small cattle raids, which was something that could be lived with.

Maina had added to his name and when Miendo died soon after—it is said from a cobra bite—the Bukusu made Maina their war leader.

Now about this time there was a young man named Chekuli who did a notable thing that earned him instant reputation and caused a great deal of talk. This Chekuli was among a small band of age brothers who went raiding across the Great Valley into Kamasia country. There were not many of them and they hoped to earn a few cattle by cunning rather than force, for they did not plan to use their spears unless they had to.

After crossing the dry river bed in the middle of the

valley they climbed the slope into Baringo and stayed some days in the forest, skulking about the glades where the Kamasia grazed their herds. But they had no luck, for the beasts were closely guarded.

Tired of empty bellies and cold nights, they set off for home with glum faces. But on their return journey to the valley floor a piece of good luck waited. They met a small herd of Kamasia cattle being driven down to a salt lick by a grown youth and two boys. The boys fled at the first sight of trouble, but the youth put up his spear until he saw more clearly the numbers to be dealt with; then he ran after the boys.

So now they had a useful herd for their pains. They were pleased with themselves and began droving across the valley as quickly as possible, hoping to get back to Mumalo unscathed. The part of the sport they embarked on now is, as everyone knows, the most hazardous. Cattle can be driven only so fast and must do some grazing if they are to survive. It was especially true of these, which had steep slopes to climb. The Kamasia would not be ignorant of this either and it was certain that there would be some pursuit.

They herded earnestly into the night, then slept a few hours with sentries straining eyes and ears while the beasts grazed, and moved again before it was light. An hour before dawn saw them across the river bed with the west wall of the valley plain in front. They were optimistic about the way things were going.

It was here Chekuli discovered that he had left a simi where they had slept the night before. It was a handily balanced blade that he was fond of, and Chekuli was not so rich a man that he could afford to lose it. He made up his mind to go back and find the weapon. Alone, he judged it would not take him long. When he explained the plan to his age brothers, they were willing that he should go but said they would not wait for him.

Chekuli recrossed the river bed by the shortest route, passing on his right hand the northern mouth of the great gorge, and made for the previous night's camping place. But before he reached it he noticed men ahead of him. They were Kamasia warriors in full war gear, about a dozen of them, and he was marked as soon as he saw them. He turned and started to run back the way he had come and the Kamasia raised one shout and then loped after him silently.

When the first shock of the meeting had settled, Chekuli began to have confidence that things might yet turn out well. He had some hard running to do before reaching the river and more before he caught up with his age brothers, but he was a notable runner who did not think it beyond his powers to stay ahead of most men, and the Kamasia were a good way behind. Also there were not so many of them that it would matter much if they were still on his heels when he did get back to the Bukusu.

He settled down to run steadily and hoard his strength, looking back over his shoulder at times to see how he was doing. The Kamasia followed faithfully enough, but it puzzled Chekuli somewhat that they were not making greater effort.

In a little while this casualness was explained. A group of four men appeared ahead to his right and began closing in. He changed direction away from them, quickened his stride, and began to take a more serious view of the problem. But still it seemed to him that the pursuit on both sides was somewhat lazy.

A minute or so later what had been dark to him was made clear. The gorge lay ahead. His changed direction had taken him some distance from where it flattened to the river crossing. And there were four men who could reach it before he had a chance of passing them.

Behind him there was a single shout of laughter. Those who followed spread out to the left to cut him off on that side and then slowed to a confident walk.

Chekuli ran until the depths gaped at his feet. He looked down. The walls of the gorge were upright, like the sides of a house, but far higher than ten house walls. They were of black rock which old torrents had worn smooth. In the dim light below, the river bed wound like a snake. He looked across, and the opposite wall was a good four spears' length away and slightly higher than where he stood.

Then he straightened up, took off the skin he wore and the leather bag hanging from his shoulder, and flung them both across the gap. He followed this with his spear and it clattered on the rock on the other side. This done, he walked back naked toward the oncoming Kamasia. But when he had gone thirty paces in their direction he turned again, ran with all his strength to the gorge, and jumped.

Certainly he was lucky in the place chosen, for here the gorge was at its narrowest; to either side it more than doubled in width. Even so, men who know the story have looked at that gap ever since and marveled. For Chekuli jumped the gorge.

He did not land cleanly; indeed he missed the lip and clung to it with every finger a claw. Then he pulled himself up, crawled over the edge and sat panting. As the Kamasia drew near he got to his feet and limped to pick up his spear and other gear. Standing back, out of reach of anything but a long spear throw, it seemed to Chekuli that he had little to worry about. A spear he could see coming and dodge.

But the Kamasia showed no signs of throwing anything. They came to the edge of the gorge and stared down, then they looked at him with respect and sat on the ground.

"Are you a man or a bird, Mkusu?" they asked.

"It's true that there's a certain quality about my jumping," replied Chekuli, "but I wouldn't say that it was by any means unusual where I live."

"A good spear throw might settle your business," said one of the band sourly.

"And they certainly look like good spears to me," said Chekuli. "I'd welcome one to take home with me. I'm by no means rich, and a good spear is never to be despised."

"That had also crossed my mind," said the Kamasia.

"I never think little of anyone's intelligence unless it's forced on me," remarked Chekuli politely.

"Perhaps there are others who can also jump."

Chekuli gave this his full attention.

"You ought to throw your spear across first, as I did," he said. "Otherwise, hampered with it, you might not do so well. I'll be glad to welcome you when you arrive; a hand may be needed."

"And what if several of us jump at the same time?"

"Now that *will* be interesting to watch," said Chekuli.

A certain kind of silence fell upon them.

"Well," said Chekuli at last, "I've enjoyed our talk but I think I'd better be getting back to my people. There are enough of them to welcome you hospitably if you should choose to join us, but they'll be busy herding, and one good man more is always welcome when it comes to that work."

And he limped away.

He had not gone far before someone shouted after him.

"Mkusu!"

"I hear you," said Chekuli.

"May we know your name?"

Chekuli told them and added, "Why do you ask?"

"This place has no name that I know of. Yours might serve to fix it in men's minds."

And indeed it is said that the Kamasia named the place after Chekuli.

The respite that Maina gained for his people by cunning did not last. They stayed to sow two more crops at Mumalo but then the times were such that it seemed wiser to leave. First, the harvests they took were poor ones, the millet dwarfish and bitten by a red blight that rotted the ears. It seemed to many that the spirits of the unknown dead who were buried there tainted the place and there was no known way of appeasing them. Also it grew plain that the Kamasia were only the locust or two found on the leaf at morning, to warn the wise man of the host that would follow in the afternoon. The tribes were pouring south again from Ethiopia—the Elgeyo, Marakwet, Tugen, and Suk—and Mumalo lay in their path. The Bukusu were increasingly troubled by raids and petty battles, and more and more they had the worst of it. They lost men, cattle, and women, and the warriors grew to dread the red-painted men from the north and were reluctant to stand against them.

So after two years Maina led the Bukusu south to Namarere. In the end he had not been successful against the Kamasia (for these new tribes were their kinsmen), but he had kept the people together and they did not blame him for failure. There were too many enemies.

It is better to pass quickly over the next few years for it was a bleak time. At Namarere there was sickness of both cattle and men. The beasts' legs swelled at the joints and were tender; they staggered in the pasture, foamed at the mouth, and died, and the pestilence would not go away. If the dead stock was eaten those who fed on it often died, and died badly. So they stayed at Namarere only long enough to reap one crop, then they fled to Murongoro and lived among steep hills and forests. But here they found a people who rolled rocks down on them from the hilltops. Although these people would not stand against a large force, vanishing like lice in a bed skin among trees and hills, they would hunt small parties with arrows slight as straws but poisoned and deadly. It is not known what tribe this was, perhaps the Terik.

So the Bukusu moved again, circling back toward the mountain, first to Silungusa and then, after crossing the Nzoia River, to Ebukaya. Something should be said at greater length about this last move.

At Silungusa there was peace of a kind, and the people, weary and depleted in numbers, began to hope their troubles would diminish, but Maina was not satisfied. He had grown in adversity and the space he held now in men's respect was large indeed. There were other strong men living at the time, but in Maina's kraal there was never room for two bulls. To those who elbowed him he taught respect. A few hived off from the tribe and took their following elsewhere, but most stayed and spoke quietly and were careful not to clutter Maina's path.

He was restless at Silungusa. He argued that this was only another place like the rest, into which they had come because they had to. All about them the tribes were boiling like a cooking pot and it was only too likely it might spill their way. However, they had to harvest what had been sown when they first came or starve, so while the women cultivated he took such men as could safely be spared and led them to Ebukaya.

Ebukaya must have looked good to these people after the bitter years. Most of it was a broad valley surrounded by thickly wooded hills. South of this the river ran sluggishly, checked by marshes and great curves so that yearly it flooded and refreshed the soil. There were birds and game in plenty, buck in the valley bottom, pig among the reeds and elephant in the forest. North was Masaba, a great back hunched against any squalls of adversity from that direction, and the reed beds and small rocky hills dotting the valley made the place one that would confuse and upset an invader.

True, Ebukaya was cluttered by a small clan of a people called the Samia, but they were few and timid. The Samia have never shown much heart for fighting and they will sell their children's land for peace. The Bukusu killed a few and others packed their traps and fled as far south, it is said, as the Great Lake. Certainly today there are people beside the lake whose squat bodies and thick wits recall to mind the Samia. But not all the Samia fled; some stayed in the valley.

Now it seemed to Maina that although he had dealt with the living, it could well happen that the ghosts of the Samia dead would be resentful, active, and bothersome. The past had taught him to be wary of haste, and he determined that at first they would only camp on the land to test the strength of its resentment. Also he wanted to find out how those Samia who remained would stomach being tenants on soil they had once owned. So although he himself went back to Silungusa, a brother called Wakulunya was left with a garrison of young men. Maina talked for a long time with Wakulunya before he left and the man took the advice that was given and showed that he possessed both prudence and resourcefulness.

The warriors built shelters on the hillside overlooking the valley and bled the Samia below of a dole of fish, grain, and occasionally a goat. Wakulunya kept these demands within reason because he did not want to drive valuable tenants to rebellion. He also did what he could to keep his young men away from Samia women. The warriors grumbled but Wakulunya turned a bleak face to their complaints and had enough of his brother's authority so that what he ordered was done. As it turned out, there was ample leisure for hunting and they found that the Samia were willing to lend them a woman or so in return for a share of a kill. Indeed the Samia girls were themselves willing to please for payment of this kind, the Samia men being slack hunters of meat.

After living for a year like this, the warriors broke a small field in the valley and sowed it with millet and beans. They kept monkeys and pig away from the growing plants and watched to see what harvest they got. It was a good one, they had never seen better, and indeed no kind of setback was experienced during this period of trial.

To Wakulunya it seemed probable that the land would

not reject them and he sent reports to Maina saying this. Maina was pleased, but still cautious. He called together the Chetung'eng'i laibons and consulted the ancestors through them, and still the omens were very good.

Now no man can ever be completely sure of anything, but Maina felt he had done all he could. Accordingly, after the harvest, the tribe left Silungusa with their possessions and stock. They poured into Ebukaya, and there was a busy time building houses and settling quarrels over land. Maina built his own house near the swamp where the soil was rich, with a papyrus swamp guarding one flank and a hill called Kilikazi the other.

He left the Samia alone on the far side of the swamp and the narrow strip of good land across the river. They proved valuable tenants and, when stiffened by Bukusu, not to be ignored at spear work. Indeed, soon the Bukusu began to marry Samia daughters, for they held the tribe of their wives to be of no account so long as the women were strong in the fields, gave pleasure at night, and bred. Maina saw that bride prices were paid for the girls, which pleased the Samia, and they became his firm allies. Indeed, a great deal of respect came to Maina from all sides, for he had promised the Bukusu good land and kept his promise.

Maina had many wives during his lifetime; truly it can be said that here was a man who liked women. It might also be added that he got little return for the trouble he spent on them. By the time they reached Ebukaya he had married twice. One wife was the Babukusu woman of whom some mention has already been made; for the other he paid bride wealth to the Teso. When he was comfortable and secure in his new home, he looked around for another wife. Partly he did this because, in common with most men, his appetite for women grew with his wealth, and Maina's herd had increased greatly; but also he had not yet fathered a child and this had begun to gnaw at his sense of fitness, as indeed it must with any man. Probably there was a certain amount of talk about this among those who followed him. Not that it was likely that any man would have mocked him to his face. Maina was open and easy with all honest men, but he hated to be diminished in any way. His anger was beginning to be feared and men were careful what they said to him, but this would not protect him from overhearing what was not intended to come his way.

For whatever reason it was, Maina wanted another wife, and it was natural that he should look no farther than among his Samia tenants. They were not forbidden to him by blood and it was likely to prove cheaper, for dependents do not force too hard a bargain when setting a bride price, especially when the prospective husband is a Maina.

So his eye fell upon a Samia girl named Akin and he married her. She could have been perhaps fifteen years of age when Maina built her a house inside his hedge but she was a woman of unusual beauty. She did not want to marry him and had only done so after some beating by her brothers, who were anxious for the cattle they would gain. However, once married she made no further fuss and took her apron off whenever he wished, and this was often enough in the first few months they were together. Not only was Maina anxious for a child but also he was made somewhat foolish by her beauty.

Now not long after the final heifer which seals the marriage had been paid, some news came to Maina. In the ojuok hedge that surrounds a great household such as his, there is always a private opening as well as the main one that is closed by thorn branches and guarded at night. It is a small tunnel through the hedge and usually situated behind the great hut of the senior wife. It is a convenient thing to have, for should a man wish to leave his compound casually at night it saves the trouble of shifting the pile of brush at the main entrance. Also it has sometimes been the means of upsetting an enemy when he thought himself in safe occupation and the fight over. It is a path that can only be used by a goat or a sheep or a man creeping on his hands and knees.

The way in which Maina heard his news was like this. He was drinking with visiting clan leaders and some private followers and, as the night passed and all there were far gone in drink, someone babbled, "There is a kind of two-legged animal who uses the small entrance to our host's household at night. He comes without invitation, though whether to share the comfort of the fire that burns there or to warm himself in some other way isn't for me to say."

Nobody made any comment on this and since at the time several men were speaking at once and all deep in the beer, it is possible that the words went unnoticed, or if they were heard, that neither speaker nor listeners remembered them for sore heads the next day.

Except Maina.

Among his personal followers there were two men who were close to him. One was named Wanyongo, an age brother of Maina's who had never come by any luck on his own account and had been content to sell his spear in return for a place in the household. The other was called Tenge, a Teso by birth and an outcast from his tribe for some reason which he was never anxious to talk about. Both of these men were content to do as they were told in order to save the trouble of worrying for themselves, and both were loyal to Maina but had few scruples about anything else.

Maina took them aside and talked for some time and after this they cut sticks forked at the end in a certain way and went to the top of the hill called Kilikazi, which lay a little to the west of the household. The long flat top of Kilikazi was covered with bald rocks and it was a notable place for snakes, who enjoyed the heat that grew in the rocks by day and lasted there into the night. Also, the hill was populated by lizards and hyrax, upon which the snakes fed. Wanyongo and Tenge caught a snake there with their forked sticks. It was one of the thick-bodied, yellow tribe, very slow except when striking, and then its bite is usually final. It was the largest of its kind that they could find and they brought it down at evening tied with thongs to a spear shaft. They dug the ground in the small entrance through the hedge and, after running a thin sharp stick through the snake's body near the tail end and weighting this with stones, they buried it there with only the head and half an arm's length of its body free.

Now here things can be left for a while to explain about a man whose name was Jusali. He was an outsider, belonging neither to the six clans nor to the Samia. A fugitive, he was thought to have come from as far away as the Baganda. When he arrived at Ebukaya he was thin and had a half-healed spear wound beneath his ribs. He had sheltered first among the Samia and, when he was somewhat recovered from his hardships, had appeared before Maina and asked for the right to build a hut, plant a garden, and fish.

Maina had looked at him for a long time. Jusali was lean but his frame was that of a tall and powerful man who did not appear to have been afraid of much in his life. He could make a valuable follower. So when he had considered, Maina said, "You can have tenant's right on a piece of land near the river."

In this way he gained another spear but did not rob his clansmen, for a squatter's brats cannot inherit. Jusali took the gift and stayed. Although with better eating he grew to be a man upon whom women were glad to rest their eyes, he was also proud and quarrelsome. However, Maina said nothing, although he kept his eye upon him.

Now, returning to the matter of the snake, Wanyongo and Tenge waited for two nights and on the morning of the second there was a man face down in the entrance. Tenge made the discovery and when he turned the body over it took a little time to recognize Jusali, the face was so swollen. Tenge brought the news discreetly to Maina. He said that he did not think the man had enjoyed his death.

Since Jusali had no clan or family to be reckoned with, the death could not possibly have been cheaper. Wanyongo and Tenge buried him quietly in an anteater's hole and there was no talk about the matter.

If indeed it was Akin he had been visiting, she carried things off most skillfully. She made no outcry and appeared to be quite unconcerned when Maina told her the news of

Jusali's death. He questioned her privately but it soon seemed that he would not get far in this direction. It would be unwise to inquire elsewhere if he did not want to become a laughing stock. So he let things lie as they were, but it was observed that afterward he felt nothing more for Akin and would have little to do with her.

So the story stops here, or perhaps it does not quite. For some time later Akin had a child who was named Simiyu. Maina recognized his son but there was never much pride heard in his voice when he spoke about him. Simiyu was the only child Maina was to have and some thought it possible that it was Jusali's seed that quickened Akin.

In Ebukaya the Bukusu felt themselves to be secure. Their way of living changed somewhat, because with a more settled life they broke greater fields than had been their custom before. Millet, both the ordinary kind and finger millet, they grew in profusion, and also, when they had been there for the time it takes an age group to come to manhood, they began planting maize. The new crop grew well in the black soil of the valley, twice as tall as a man during good years. The women grumbled a little over grinding the new grain, for it was far harder than millet, but since maize yielded more heavily and the porridge and cake made from it satisfied hunger much longer, the complaint was halfhearted. Many children were born and lived; the growing clans pushed into empty land to the west and north and also up the lower slopes of the mountain.

There was only one small piece of grit between the toes of those who lived at Ebukaya, and it was that in some years the rain was fitful. At these times the storms hung black upon the mountain; the thunder echoed in the deep-slashed gorges above, and then went away, leaving the valley dry when the land all around was sodden. It was not a misfortune that occurred every year, only occasionally, but when it did hardship followed.

Now one day a stranger arrived in Ebukaya, and his only companion was a large bull with wide-spreading, wickedly sharp horns. He came from the south and the young men stopped him among the border farms and brought him to Maina. Somewhat fatter and less active than he had been in youth, the chief was sitting on a stool in the shade of his hedge when the stranger and his beast were brought before him. Maina looked first at the bull, which was black and white and bigger than any bull he had seen before. The Bukusu value a black-and-white animal above all others. Then he turned his attention to the man, who seemed not at all impressed by the young men with spears who herded him or by the importance of Maina upon his stool.

Maina asked him his name.

"Mulembe," he was told.

"Where do you come from, Mulembe, and why are you here?"

Mulembe pointed southwest and said that he came from Marachi, a name which no one there had ever heard before.

"As to your second question," continued Mulembe, "I came this way because of an argument I had with a certain man. It was a dispute that I both won and lost. He proposed to take certain liberties with the ownership of this bull you see here and I questioned his right. I won because I pushed my spear through his guts and after that his interest in the discussion waned. I lost because he had a clan who would certainly have done the same thing to me if they'd got the opportunity. I came away to stop further argument."

"It is a fine bull," remarked Maina.

"Now there you speak the truth," said Mulembe. "The man I speared, however, made a similar remark at the beginning of our conversation. I hope you're not going to take the same course as he did, because I don't want any more trouble."

"It doesn't seem to me," said Maina, "that you're well placed to make threats. If I were you I'd speak a little more delicately."

"I'm not threatening anyone," said Mulembe. "I'm just explaining what I have to do when people get mistaken ideas about who owns this bull."

Maina looked at the bull again and then at the man and he still did not know which he liked better.

"Listen," he said, "and if you can manage it, hold your tongue until I've finished. My heart goes out for that bull as it rarely goes out for anything these days, but also I must confess a certain liking for you. Apart from that, you're a stranger and seem to have come peacefully, and we're not in the habit of harming men who do that. 'Mukini wayangala embwa'—A visitor should not be beaten. Neither should he be robbed. Now in my opinion there's just one way out of this conflict between what I should do and what I want to do."

"Sounds more and more like the one I speared," said Mulembe to no one in particular.

"I think it would be best," went on Maina, "if you stayed here and let your bull run with my herd. If he's as good at his occupation as he looks to me, he should get a fair number of my cows with his calves and some of them may resemble their father. So I might achieve what I want in that way. However, that lies in the future and is uncertain, and meanwhile the bull grazes my land, and you, since I don't think you'll be parted from him, eat my porridge. For these things I consider it fair that you pay a little in service. I need a kraal herdsman and guard. Will you stay and sweep dung for me?"

"I was mistaken," said Mulembe. "A much better proposal than the other one made, and most certainly I'll accept it. However, we must speak further about those calves you talked of. To my way of thinking some of them should belong to me."

"Khakaba!" said Maina. "You bargain harder than a Teso."

"My people have been known to get a fair price for their own droppings," said Mulembe modestly.

So Mulembe became kraal herdsman to Maina, carried the dung in winnowing baskets from the kraal floor to the midden each day, and took his turn beside the guard fire at night. The rest of the time he slept, played pebble draughts, and filled himself with porridge like anyone else. He did one thing that was different, however. Each evening when the herd returned to the kraal he conversed fondly with his bull. He scratched between its horns, gently rubbed the wet black nose, and searched for gorged blue ticks among the soft folds beneath its chin. And while he did these things he spoke to it in a private language of his own. Whether the bull replied in the same tongue is unknown, for on these occasions Mulembe preferred to be alone, staring hard at any observers and waiting in silence until they had gone.

Now the rainy season following Mulembe's arrival was just such a one as has been described. Time and time again, heavy rain-breeding clouds gathered and promised. Rain in plenty fell upon the mountain; it stayed shrouded for days, and the rivers flowing from it ran in spate. There were reports of generous rains and early planting in Teso and on the plains, but in Ebukaya, nothing. Finally the skies cleared, and the crater above was sharp-etched for all to see before it vanished in a haze of heat. Manifestly, the seasons of this year had become confused, and men tried to avoid looking at the months of famine that surely lay ahead.

One day a herdboy brought news to Maina, and when he had heard the child out, his face hardened with anger and he set off to walk to the herd. What he found there did not please him at all. His own great bull lay dead, gored between the ribs, with the flies clotting the black wounds. Somewhat apart, the eldest of its sons, an animal upon which Maina doted, struggled to regain its feet. Its loins were broken and useless and the guts spilled from its ripped belly.

Backed against a clump of papyrus, the murderer bellowed and cleansed its horns, rubbing them first right and then left on the turf. No man there would go near; it was the black-and-white stranger.

They fetched Mulembe, and he gentled the bull's nose, led it home, and tied it by the horns to the fence outside the kraal. Then Maina and Mulembe faced each other.

"The bull must die," said Maina bluntly.

"Then so must I, and it's possible I won't go alone," replied Mulembe.

"Can you make blood payment?" asked Maina.

"For two bulls! You know I have nothing except my own bull."

"Then how can this matter be settled?"

"I don't see it settled," said Mulembe. "You must understand that I'm not arguing but I don't see any satisfaction for anyone here. All I know is that if Katondwe dies, I'll die with him, and perhaps we'll take someone with us."

"Who's Katondwe?" asked Maina.

"My bull."

"I didn't know," said Maina.

They stood there in silence for a long time, two good men wrestling with an intolerable problem. At last Maina stirred and was about to speak when Mulembe raised his hand.

"Wait a little longer," he begged. "It's possible that I see a way out of this trap we've both fallen into."

So Maina called for beer and his stool and they drank together. Then Mulembe spoke.

"Listen," he said, "and you might have that pot you're drinking from replenished before I begin, because I've a great deal to explain and it will take time."

So Maina did as had been suggested and when he was comfortable, his lips well moistened and fly whisk to hand, Mulembe began.

"My people," he said, "are called the Bunyore. We're a small people who live inland from the Great Lake and we've little reputation except in two directions. One is for idleness. Mungu! but we lie late abed in Bunyore, and why not, for our land is fertile and needs few men to tend it, and the hills don't make it easy for strangers to call. The other is for the kind of magic that brings the rain. Now the idleness is a talent all our people are born with, but the rain magic is confined to one small clan called the Vagimba, who descended from a man called Mugimba. He lived a vast time ago and his story is of great interest, for it goes like this. . . ."

"I think," said Maina, "that the story of this man Mugimba should wait a little since, as you say, he lived a long time ago, whereas our problem is here and now."

"Perhaps you're right," said Mulembe. "Yes, certainly it would be wiser to let it lie for the time being. It's a pity though, because there are aspects of this story which could be guaranteed to interest anybody, but there, put it aside. Remind me, when all this is over, to tell it to you. The point is that all the Vagimba can bring the rain to some degree, though certainly, some of them are more practiced than others. It's not a question of ability, you understand—all Vagimba have that—but of inclination of which talent to exploit, for the idleness is in them also and many prefer to explore along that path. There's a great deal of work connected with rain making."

Maina sighed deeply into his beer. "I don't see that we're getting any closer to the matter in hand," he said. "To have postponed Mugimba was good, but now he's multiplied into a whole clan of Vagimba, and I still have two fine beasts lying dead whose blood calls out for recompense."

"But surely," protested Mulembe, "now you see the door out of the hut?"

"I'm still in darkness," declared Maina.

"But I belong to the Vagimba clan."

"That's the second thing I didn't know," said Maina heavily. "Why didn't you say so?"

"I thought I did," said Mulembe. "I meant to. Surely I . . ."

"Never mind," said Maina hastily. "So, being a Vagimba, you can bring the rain. Why didn't you declare this before? Here's much of the land drying up when it should be running with water and everyone thinking of famine to come, while among us sits a man who claims to be able to unloose the rain. Practice that art successfully, my friend, and you'll certainly find many who'll be prepared to make your blood payment for you."

"There's still a small obstacle in the way," said Mulembe, "and it is this. Obviously I can make it rain if you want me to, but in order to do so I require certain drugs, charms, magic objects. They aren't all there is to it, of course—the talent is the main thing—but I certainly couldn't assume success without these other aids I mentioned. Now, as I've explained, I left Bunyore in somewhat hurried circumstances—I did explain that, didn't I? I think I . . ."

"You explained," said Maina. "And I take it, due to those same hurried circumstances, you left your charms behind."

"Unfortunately."

"And now you want to return and get them?"

"That's right."

"Hmm," said Maina.

"Yes," said Mulembe and sighed as silence fell between them.

Presently Maina stirred.

"The bull would have to stay here," he said. "Yes, certainly that would have to remain."

"I knew you'd think so," said Mulembe sadly. "Eh, it'll be a wrench and how he'll manage without me I can't begin to imagine. However, I suppose it has to be. It would be a kindness, though, if while I'm away someone would talk to him a little during the evening. Won't be the same, of course, but perhaps by this time he's begun to understand something of the language you speak here. And he doesn't like the ticks clustered beneath his chin."

"I'll do it myself," said Maina.

"Thank you," said Mulembe. "You're an attractive man. And now I must go and explain to Katondwe why I'm going to Bunyore. I shall be some time about this journey; it won't be an easy one. Don't make any rash decisions about Katondwe because you believe I'm not returning. The curse of a Vagimba is not something to be trifled with."

He did not begin his journey that day. It was overlate; there was a bag of food to be begged, and other small matters to arrange. But he went the next morning and was gone about ten days, and during that time Maina went to the kraal each evening to play Mulembe's role with Katondwe. It became something that was talked about, and men would walk a fair distance to manage accidentally to be in sight when Maina was picking ticks off the large black-and-white bull. And the strange thing was that the presence of witness seemed to have precisely the same effect upon him as it had on Mulembe. He glowered until whoever was watching went hastily away.

When Mulembe returned he looked thinner and carried a skin bag of mysteries. He spoke with his bull and then slept for many hours. But the next day he was out and busy, eyeing the mountain, snuffing the wind, rattling with a little stick upon the hard red walls of the ant heaps and listening to any answering flutter from the creatures within. He was followed by a silent and curious crowd, of which he took no notice.

This continued for two days and then he climbed to the top of Kilikazi and settled for a long time upon a rock, staring north at the bulk of Masaba. Suddenly he smiled, nodded his head, and muttered something to himself. That done, he opened the bag. He had taken out a stoppered gourd and a few snake bones when he seemed at last to become aware of the watching crowd, and he gave them the stony stare that previously had been used to drive off those who eavesdropped on the conversations with Katondwe. Mulembe's eyes were strangely direct for one usually so vague about everyday matters; his audience found themselves uncomfortable and went hurriedly down the hill. So no one knew exactly what Mulembe did, but he stayed on the hill the whole of that day and night and in the morning came down looking sleek. And two days later the clouds gathered on Masaba and in the evening rolled in a wall across Ebukaya. The weather broke no promises this time and in a week people were grumbling about leaking thatch and wet beds.

But they were grateful. Mulembe made his blood payment to Maina and had plenty besides to begin on a piece of land the elders granted him. They also gave him several girls to marry, and in time he had many children. His descendants today are a small clan still famous among the Bukusu for rain making; they are called the BaMulembe. Mulembe himself, however, practiced the art only for as long as he was forced to. When his eldest son was grown and skilled enough to conjure the rain, his father thankfully handed over the task. Then, usually in the shade of a hut, with a pot of beer to hand, Mulembe devoted himself to the first of his two talents.

Maina's wife Akin died when her son Simiyu was a grown boy. After her death he married a number of women taken from his Samia tenants, but the children he craved escaped him. The tale of Maina's marriages grows repetitive and tiresome; a new hut would be built within the hedge and for a year the new wife would occupy it. Then Maina would despair and angrily send her back to her family as a barren and useless creature and demand the return of the bride wealth. During the haggling about this a father, uncle, or brother of the girl would try to suggest, delicately, wrapping his words with care, that might it not be the husband rather than the wife? The question would hang, impalpable as a cobweb, and the man who made it would stare at his hands, at a passing cloud, at a dog scratching fleas in the bare compound, at anything but the bulky, aging Maina simmering with fury before him.

Then Maina would turn and glare significantly at his son, Simiyu, whom he always contrived to have standing beside him on these occasions. Nothing was said, Maina would not chance that, just the look. The man before Maina would search for words which could make what he longed to say acceptable, and the courage to express them, and decide not. After an uncomfortable silence the discussion would resume about the calf that one of the bride-price cows had dropped the season before and . . .

Always after this a time would follow when Maina

peered out of a dark, stormy world, one in which men avoided him if they had the choice. They would not even drink with him. Simiyu shouldered his affairs and made such decisions about the household as were needed until his father emerged, bloated and shaking from the beer, but having found his way to a new hope. There would be another hut built inside the hedge, another Samia girl to occupy it—until such time as the whole business had to be repeated. Tcha!

After three of these domestic upheavals there was a lull in marriages for several years. The two first wives, aging women now, managed the household, a number of Samia girls provided pleasure, but his main interest was in cattle. The times were peaceful and the herds grew unwieldy, Maina's among them. Cattle in such quantities could not run for long in one place without exhausting the grass, and Maina divided his beasts into two herds and grazed the larger in distant empty country to the south. Too far to be brought back at night, they required a strong guard of herdsmen and Simiyu commanded these, stayed with the cattle, and lived hard.

A little must now be said about this Simiyu whom Maina called a son. He was a man of promise, tall and strong, lighter-skinned than most Bukusu, a red man. Life bubbled in him; he was always hunting, drinking, playing with women, laughing, a man of easy authority whom others followed without question. There was little occupation for his spear but he looked for it whenever he had the chance, slipping away to raid with the Chetung'eng'i, who liked him. He was disgruntled because Maina kept him tied to the cattle. There was no love between this father and son;

Simiyu's name for his father was "Beer-pot," and Maina preferred his son out of sight. Also Maina was reluctant to let him marry and when asked about this growled, "Earn a name before you busy yourself with women. That's what I did."

Simiyu would have it that the Beer-pot grudged him the cattle for bride wealth.

"That worn-out old goat would sooner part with his cods than a cow," he declared to his drinking companions. And added, "Not that anyone would get a bargain there, for his cods never proved to be up to much."

Now this state of affairs had endured for a time when Maina took it into his head to try again and married another wife. A Samia girl like the rest, she was named Batilu, young and very beautiful. Whether she wanted Maina as a husband is questionable but her family was greedy for the bride wealth, so she had little choice. A quiet, docile girl, she took her place in the household, deferring to the elder wives, and seeming concerned only to please. Maina was infatuated, praised the food she cooked, spent his nights in her new house, and was restless if she moved far from him. An old man now, he had grown lonely and did not find it easy to open his heart with anyone. But to Batilu he warmed and, seeing them together, men often remarked that they appeared more like father and deeply loved daughter than man and wife.

When the marriage occurred Simiyu was absent with the cattle, but with the rains and ample grass growing, they were brought back to the valley. There followed three lazy months for herdsmen. Two boys could do the work by day and at night the beasts slept safely inside the kraals near the household. The place was populous with idle young men; there was dancing and drumming in the villages and storytelling at night.

After a time one of Maina's hangers-on, it might have been Wanyongo or perhaps Tenge, mentioned in a roundabout way that the friendship of Simiyu with his stepmother was a pleasing thing to see. Taking note of this, Maina began to study them both.

One morning he looked for Batilu and could not find her. When he inquired, he was told she had gone to a hill called Babuya beyond the swamp and near the house of her kinsman Sanjamolo. She had left at dawn, intending to gather some lily bulbs that grew there whose bitterness was good for the stomach and whose red sap made a striking dye in a grass mat. Maina was satisfied, but then another thought came to him and he asked for Simiyu. No one could say where he was, perhaps with the cattle near the swamp, or spearfishing higher up the river.

Maina fidgeted out the morning and in the afternoon took his stool and sat by the kraal fence, watching the grass lands toward the river. At evening he saw his wife and son a long way off. They were too distant for him to be certain but he thought that they walked hand in hand. When they reached the kraal they were not touching, but there was a sleekness on both of them he had not noticed before.

Batilu greeted him easily and he asked her where she had been. She told him to her kinsman's house and on to Babuya gathering lily roots.

"And where have *you* been?" he asked Simiyu.

His son smiled and asked, "Do you think it is wise that your wife should travel so far alone? Surely it wouldn't please either of us if she'd been taken by a leopard, and there are crocodiles this year at the river crossing. I met her this morning when I was going to the cattle. Since there was nothing pressing to do I went with her to Babuya."

"And where are these lily bulbs?" asked Maina.

Batilu showed him a small basket half full. They seemed to be too few for a long day's gathering and Maina said so.

"Yes, there weren't so many as I remembered," she said carelessly. "But Sanjamolo said the wild pig had increased and certainly there were signs of digging all over the hill. Simiyu says the place might give a day's hunting. He and Sanjamolo made plans for it."

Then she went singing to her house to prepare the lily bulbs and both the men in their separate ways watched her go.

Maina drank heavily for the rest of that day and the next morning also. In the afternoon he sent a child to Batilu with word that he would eat her cooking that night and later, when the smoke from the house fires hung between the huts, he went to her compound. She knelt and greeted him with softly clapping hands and he looked in vain for any hint of mockery. He was brought stiff millet cake over which was poured a stew of fish and pumpkin leaves, and while he ate she watched him from a little distance. The food was good and he was fond of fish but the beer was sour in his throat and he ate little.

"My cooking doesn't please you tonight," said Batilu as she gathered up the crocks.

"No," he replied, "it was good, but I'm not hungry."

"It happens that way sometimes," she said.

He looked at her with sadness and anger and desire so

mixed that he would have been hard put to say which was uppermost.

"We will go to your sleeping mat," he said and then added quickly, "if you want me there, that is."

She said quietly and without any kind of emphasis, "The child said you would eat with me, and you've done so, although it's true the food didn't seem greatly to your taste. After feeding her man, a wife expects him to play the husband."

She moved before him into the hut, stooping beneath the looped-up door skin. He dropped it full behind them and stood in the half-light watching her. She took a bed kaross and threw it over the sleeping mat, then slipped off her apron and stretched out naked and open on the kaross.

After a little while, when he had not moved, she asked, "Is it the same with me as it was with the food, that you're not hungry?"

"Perhaps you don't want me to be?" he asked.

Batilu laughed. "No," she said, "but again, sometimes it happens."

"That you don't want me?"

"There's something in you tonight that makes you want to twist my words. I meant that I'm not wanted."

"You might prefer another."

"Eh! How could that be? I'm your wife; the bride price was paid."

"Now there at last is truth," he said and went clumsily, an old man shaking with foolish desire and anger, to the mat. While he groped for her he searched for some sign of reluctance he could have read as proof, but found only calm obedience. Finished, he thrust her away, huddled into his robe and left the hut. If a laugh had followed him he would have returned and killed her, but there was only the silence of secrecy.

So this was how life was for these three. Simiyu and Batilu moved always discreetly separate, but with the same luxury upon them both. When Simiyu listened to his father's instruction it seemed to Maina that he did so with a weighted, serious deference that giggled underneath. Batilu seemed to have the smell of Simiyu on her and it killed desire. When Maina was alone he knew he was old.

Then one night he went late to Batilu's house, pushed aside the door skin, and found them sleeping beneath a single kaross. He went stumbling back across the worn earth of the compound, but fell before he reached his own house. He lay there in the cold and was found by his other wives with soil stuck to the spittle that smeared his mouth. They took him inside and sat him on his stool—a chieftain's chair which only he could use, called Simbi yo Mukasa—wiped his mouth and clucked. He sat there for a long time in silence and they were afraid to question him.

At last he stirred and told them to send for the clan elders of the Bukusu.

By noon the next day all the elders were assembled.

Masaba of Maina's clan had been there since dawn, for their lands shared boundary marks. Cherono of the Omufuini, Mungoma of the Omubichachi, and Walemba from the Omwahala soon followed, for their kraals were close by in the valley. Maina greeted them sparsely and signaled to his wives to bring beer. Then, his face covered by a kaross, he sat still and silent upon his stool while the four elders squatted, drank the beer when it came, and waited. In the late morning they were joined by Milikwa of the Babukusu and last, for his kraal lay on the far western border, by Khunya Masai from the Chetung'eng'i. All now were gathered.

Maina sent a boy to break five small sticks from the ojuok of his hedge and, when these had been brought, to fetch his wife Batilu and his son Simiyu. While he waited he held the five wands with their broken ends downward so that the white sap in them dripped on the floor. By the time Batilu and Simiyu arrived the sticks were drained and the drying sap made a scab across each end.

"Now," said Maina, "all of you listen, for I've a problem which must be settled."

Then he bunched the wands in his left hand, selected one with his right, and pointed it toward the elders.

"First," he said, "it is well known to you all that I've a son called Simiyu, and that's one thing."

And here he threw the wand on the ground and chose another.

"Second, I've a wife named Batilu, for whom bride wealth has been paid, and that's another thing."

The second wand joined the first.

"Now it has been said to me that I should watch my son and my wife; a third. I did so and last night I found them sleeping together beneath one skin; a fourth. And so I say to all of you here, that this is confusion because my son has replaced me in the womb of my wife before I am dead. There you have the fifth and last thing."

The wands were on the floor at his feet, his hands empty, and he asked them in a whisper what he should do.

The elders considered for a while and then Khunya took a beaded snuff bag from beneath his robe, snuffed with care, and made to speak. But before he could do so, Simiyu, lounging against the door post, said, "I think that I must be allowed a word here."

Maina looked at him with hatred and growled, "What is there for you to say? You can't deny that I've spoken the truth, because I saw you with her from the doorway of the house. I'm not yet blind."

"Oh, *that,*" said Simiyu. "I dare say you spoke the truth about that, Father." His voice leaned ironically upon the last word and the great veins in Maina's neck began to beat. "But there's something else you said which might not be quite so true. As I heard it, you used the word 'confusion.' Are you so sure it can be called that?"

"Yes!" shouted Maina and his voice was thick and hoarse like that of a bull in rut. "She is my wife!" He beat his great fist on a knee and roared, "Confusion, confusion, confusion! I say it's confusion. Aren't you my son?"

"When my mother was alive she used to tell it a different way," said Simiyu.

Maina reared to his feet and stood shaking and bellowing until Masaba spoke up. He was a kinsman of Maina's, a thin, dry, finicky man with a great memory for custom and a rasping, compelling voice. That voice somehow bored into the old man's clamor and made itself heard.

"I take it," he said, "that we weren't brought here to listen to a family quarrel, but rather to judge something that affects us all. And to my way of thinking, after listening to Maina's five things, indeed that's so. The son has replaced the father, Simiyu here said as much. He didn't deny he'd been seen with the woman, and certainly evil could come of this for all of us. There's only one course to take. With the woman we should wait to see if anything grows in her womb. If she proves to be with child then it could be Simiyu's and that would be monstrous. She should not be allowed to come to term but must die with the child unborn. But if, on the other hand, there's no child, then it's simply a matter of a woman who's been opened by a man other than her husband. The husband can deal with that as he thinks fit.

"Now remains Simiyu. His case is plain also. He has replaced his father and might do the same again. He should die."

When he had finished Milikwa, who sat next to him, raised his head and said simply, "I see nothing to quarrel with in what Masaba has said. I think as he does."

Maina was quiet now, mollified by this, and he turned to Khunya and asked for his opinion. The man was old and wise, with great influence, and Maina knew that whichever way he decided the rest were likely to follow. Khunya sat for some time with bowed head considering his way and then he stood and spoke. He had a quiet voice but one that men listened to.

"Maina, it is true that your son and wife have made confusion possible, for if a child comes of this it will perplex the ancestors to know whose spirit can rightly live in it and in this uncertainty who knows what evil thing might take a place there and live among us to our harm? So what has already been said on this is right; we must wait for the outcome and deal with it as has been described. As far as this, Masaba and I walk together. For the rest, we part.

"If you kill your son, who has within him and carries the

name of an ancestor, then your crime against the dead is worse than the one Simiyu has made possible. You cannot kill a son who, as yet, has not killed. There is no case here of a life for a life."

At this, Cherono of the Omufuini spoke unasked, saying, "I also think this."

Maina turned bitterly to those who had not yet spoken but he knew what their opinion would be; in spite of his craving for Simiyu's death he still recognized wisdom when he heard it. As he thought, Mungoma and Walemba reluctantly agreed with Khunya, and Maina was outvoted.

He said, "It would have been better if I had not looked for custom in this matter but done as my heart told me. And I don't mean better for myself only, but for all of us. However, I invoked custom and must now go where it leads. The burden is on you, Khunya; are we to leave it like this or is there more to be done?"

"Yes," said Khunya, "there's more to be done. Evil is here and it calls for sacrifice. A bull must be offered to Wele by your clan. It must be a good beast; Wele will not be cheated in this. When the part due to him has been laid aside, then the rest must be eaten by every soul of the Masaba. Even children too young to eat meat must have a taste laid on their lips; no one must be missed. This done, it is possible that the thing will stop there and evil be averted. You can but try and wait and see."

"We will do that, then," said Maina. "I'll find the beast; the best in my herd, Khunya can be judge of that. I know that this touches the Masaba only and not you, but I would ask all of you to stay and see the sacrifice made. When it's over then I have a word for each of you."

The sacrifice to Wele was held the next day. In the presence of all his clan, Maina slit the throat of a white bull and it was butchered skillfully by men known to be good at this work. The heart, liver, and testicles were set aside for the god and the rest roasted over a great pit. While the meat was cooking the three pieces were carried to the river and thrown hopefully into the water. One of Wele's names is Wele kwe Luchi—the River God—and it was thought there was most hope that he would find his portion there. The blood stained the water and a crocodile was seen to take the liver before it sank from sight, which was a favorable sign. After this the clan returned to the roast and ate their shares. Each householder cried the name of everyone in his family before they ate to make certain none were missed, and even children at the breast had their lips smeared with meat.

There was a great crowd, for many people from other clans had come to watch, and all the elders remained as Maina had wished.

When it was evening and everything possible had been done, Maina stood up and reminded them of the word for each that he had promised.

To Masaba and Milikwa the Teso he said this. "Both your peoples will increase until each is greater than the rest of the clans put together. Both of you will live in your houses until the next sons born to you are as old and wise as you are now."

To the elders of the Omubichachi and Omwahala he said simply, "I can promise you nothing, either good or bad."

Cherono of the Omufuini was next and Maina told him, "None of your people will ever build for long. You will go like madmen around Masaba and if you cross Nzoia River you will die."

And last he turned to Khunya.

"For you I have this. Your clan will wander again. Wherever you've lived and left, another people will replace you, driving out the ghosts remaining. You will wither as a people and the curse won't be worked out until there's but one man left who can call himself Chetung'eng'i. Through him you may thrive again, but this I can't say. I can see no farther than that one man."

Then Maina went to his house, leaving many there worried about their future.

There is not much else to be told about Maina. He drove Simiyu out and the young man is said to have become a warrior among the Luo and gained a great reputation. Batilu did not have a child and she wept much, either because Simiyu had gone or because Maina ill-treated her. Indeed from that time on he seems to have got greater pleasure from beating her than he had previously in other ways. She outlived him and after his death went as wife to a kinsman of Maina's among the Masaba, and this husband gave her children. Perhaps she was happier then.

Maina married once more, a Babukusu woman called Nabusambia, and her end is as mysterious as his, for soon after the marriage she disappeared. It is possible that he killed her but there is no knowing the truth of this, since before her family could make inquiry, Maina also left his people forever. It may be that he left with her; we do not know. What is certain is that he took with him the royal stool, Simbi yo Mukasa, and nothing else.

During the last few years of his old age, and especially since his curse, the people had feared him greatly. But because once he had earned their love and respect, they searched for him a long time. But no trace of Maina was ever found. There is a child's story that he lives in the great crater of Masaba and that when, as occurs in some years during the cool season, the rim of the pit turns white, it is Maina peering over, for at the last his hair became white.

Nanguba

When the chieftainship had been empty for almost a year, Nanguba of the clan Masaba called some of the elders to a meeting. This Nanguba has not yet been mentioned and it is time to say something of him. A brother of Maina, though much younger, he was a powerful man who took great pleasure in eating (it is said he could demolish an entire goat at one sitting). He had lived all his life in his brother's shadow and apparently had been content to do so. Now it seemed he had ambitions and thought this the right time to achieve them. What he wanted was to be chief.

Masaba, the same Masaba who had given Maina the advice he wanted, was willing to support Nanguba in this so long as it did not involve him in too much trouble. He had always been anxious to please anyone who seemed powerful and Nanguba now had the power of great wealth. With Simiyu gone, Maina's herds, hangers-on, and tenants all had come to Nanguba. It was certain that the Masaba clan would follow these two if they were in agreement, but this was not enough. A chief must have greater support than his own clan, and the purpose of the meeting was to get it.

Nanguba thought it best to begin in a small way, and so privately he feasted Mungoma of the Omubichachi and Walemba from the Omwahala. These two were chosen because he judged them interested in wealth rather than power. There were few with a quicker eye for a man's weakness than Nanguba, and his instinct here proved right. Mungoma and Walemba promised support in return for a heavy dole of cattle if he became chief. Their common interest settled, they discussed means.

Mungoma said, "I see it this way. If we count in clans we're halfway there; but if we reckon in strength then things are far from certain. The Omufuini alone number almost as many as our three clans put together. Now with the Chetung'eng'i and Babukusu on our side we'd be better placed, so these two must be sounded out. Since, Nanguba, they're both out-clans as yours is, this should be left to you."

"There is sense in that," said Nanguba, "and I'll do it. But your reason points two ways; the Omufuini are Bukusu, as you are. You should approach Cherono."

"Cherono won't be easy," replied Mungoma. "Unless I'm mistaken his ideas are somewhat similar to yours; he wants to be chief. But certainly Walemba and I might try him."

"I have a better thought than that," said Walemba. "Let's leave Cherono's pot to cook on its own for a time. As Mungoma says, he has aspirations and there are too many spears at his call for him to feel he has to agree to anything he doesn't want to. Also, Nanguba, he's too rich to be bought as we've been, so put that thought out of your mind if you had it. Leave him alone and work at getting the other clans behind us. With them we'd be strong enough to put down the Omufuini, and that might be the best thing that could happen. There'd be wonderful pickings in land and cattle for us all. If, on the other hand, we can't persuade the Chetung'eng'i and Babukusu to join us we might at least frighten them into standing aside in this matter. Then we can wave custom at Cherono, since we're three to one."

This seemed to Nanguba the best course to follow and so, after a little inconclusive private talking with Milikwa of the Babukusu and Khunya Masai, he brought his plans more into the daylight. He arranged that the great men of the clans should meet at Emabusi. There is a hill there with steeply sloping sides of rock and on the plain below three great fig trees which grow entwined. The place appointed was beneath these.

Messages calling all the clans were sent, but Nanguba arranged that word would reach the Omufuini very late, hoping that by the time they managed to gather their people together, his business would be over. They would discover that a decision had been reached and everyone unwilling to argue the matter again.

By midmorning Nanguba, Masaba, Mungoma, and Walemba, with their elders and important warriors, were at the trees. They sat and took snuff together and some of their women cooked for them. Later Milikwa came with his Babukusu, but it was not until midday that any word came from the Chetung'eng'i. The laibon who brought it explained that they would not be coming because of some likelihood of trouble with the Teso. Khunya would prefer to stand aside from any decision made at the gathering, although he wished his laibon to return with a full report. The laibon added with a faint smile that he was quite sure so much wisdom would be assembled that they could easily do without the little the Chetung'eng'i could provide.

Nanguba stood up and said with a fine display of hurt indignation, "Very well. If they wish to throw away their right to a say in Bukusu affairs then they must hold their tongues afterward. Four of the six clans are here and it's enough. We should begin."

Then, since he did not want to appear overeager, he let Walemba take his place. Walemba was about to speak when the Chetung'eng'i laibon, whose name was Nyang'oli, interrupted him.

"Although," he said, "I am, of course, quite ignorant of the doubtless great matter which Walemba is going to put to us, don't you think it would be wise if we waited a little longer? Cherono Omufuini isn't here, and I don't think he'll want to miss what's going to be said."

Walemba said, "We've all heard that Cherono was asked to come. Obviously he has chosen not to do so. Do we have to sit here growing roots waiting for the Omufuini? Also, Nyang'oli, it appears to me that your voice isn't needed, because one man can't speak for a clan. You were sent to be a pair of ears, not a mouth."

"That's so true," said Nyang'oli, "and how well you put it. But could I be allowed just one last word before I lose my voice? Nothing was mentioned that robbed me of my eyes; could I be permitted to use them?"

"Oh, by all means," said Walemba impatiently.

"Thank you," replied Nyang'oli humbly. "I've done so. So perhaps might you."

He pointed along the valley, where they saw a large group of men coming their way. It was the Omufuini.

Cherono had brought all his elders and war leaders and a very strong backing of warriors, and many there were not pleased to see them. However, a good face was put on it and Cherono was welcomed.

"You're late," said Nanguba. "We had despaired of your coming and had almost begun."

"It's true we're late," said Cherono grimly. "Though whether we're as late as was intended is something else."

The Omufuini sat together in a group and listened to Walemba, who spoke for some time and spoke well. First he went over what was known about Maina's disappearance. He reminded them that because of their uncertainty about what had happened, it had been thought best to wait before replacing him. Now, in Walemba's opinion, they had put off things long enough, possibly too long. The people lacked a chief and were like children without a father to guide them. Someone must sit upon Maina's stool or, since he had taken it with him, some other stool (that could be discussed later). To his mind there was only one person who should do so and that was Nanguba. Everything was in his favor. Maina had been a great man, the greatest the Bukusu had ever known, and Nanguba was his brother by the same parents. It would be reasonable to believe that Maina's virtues might also lie in Nanguba. Also the ghost of Maina could not help being pleased by such a choice and they could expect it to continue to help them. There was more. Nanguba was of middle age, young enough to lead them for a long time with all his powers intact, but not so young as to lack the wisdom that comes from years. He had said enough. In his opinion, they must persuade Nanguba to take the name of chief.

"He won't need much pressing," said the laibon to nobody in particular and then apologized contritely for breaking silence. "I was carried away by Walemba's eloquence," he said.

Mungoma added his voice in support of Nanguba, and all the Omubichachi and Omwahala hastened to join in.

"If I was able to speak I would say this was most moving," said Nyang'oli. "It does one good to listen to it. So many with one voice. I wonder how it happened."

Nanguba remained silent, occasionally shaking his head with every sign of reluctance, but when they began calling for him he got slowly to his feet.

"I find it difficult to speak about this," he said fluently. "I don't wish to appear to push myself forward and yet I hear so many voices calling. What Walemba said embarrassed me, but he gave sound reasons for what he proposed. They had not occurred to me before. Against my inclination, I am almost persuaded to take Maina's place. But before I decide, I'd like to hear what the Omufuini have to say. So far they've been silent."

"Yes, indeed, you'll hear us," said Cherono briskly. "Since when have the Bukusu chosen their chief because he happened to be of the same family as the man who's gone? In the past we've followed a man who's given proof that he can lead us effectively in war. That's why Maina sat where he did, and when the fighting was over we kept him because he was as good in peace as he was in war. Can anyone tell me when Nanguba got himself a name with a spear? There's another thing also. In times of peace the chieftainship has always gone to the richest clan. If this custom is followed, then the Omufuini should get it."

Cherono sat down and his clan bunched behind him.

Nanguba spoke again, and the anger in his voice somewhat spoiled the reluctance he had shown before.

"Which in plain words," he said, "means that Cherono wants to be chief. He says that I've no reputation for fighting; what better has he? As for the chieftainship going to the richest clan, what proof is there that the Omufuini have more wealth than anyone else? Also there's a good reason why no Omufuini should be made chief of the Bukusu. It's well known that their young men no longer circumcise."

Now this last was to some extent true, and many who were listening growled approval, but Cherono was on his feet again.

"Circumcision isn't a matter for the tribe, only for the clan. The Omufuini have never all circumcised and it's never been held against them in the past. As to which clan is the wealthiest, if proof is wanted I know a customary way of showing it. Let Nanguba name a day and the Omufuini will show that they don't fear comparison with his clan, nor with the rest of you put together."

At this all the Omufuini shouted their defiance and rattled spears against shields, and it was plain that any further debate would end in fighting. But the more soberminded elders agreed upon a day and place where proof of wealth should be made.

After that they all went back to their kraals to prepare, and it was observed that Nanguba was far from satisfied. He was not the kind of man who would take quietly a set-back to his plans.

The custom that Cherono had referred to for deciding which of two parties was wealthier was known to everyone. But although old, it was rarely invoked, being impracticable except in times of plenty, and no one living had ever seen it done. So there were many who were curious to do so, and great crowds gathered on the day it took place. There would be no shortage of witnesses as to who had the better of it.

It was managed like this. The clans gathered their cattle and drove them to the plain beneath Emabusi. The Omwahala, Omubichachi, and Masaba herded their beasts together on one side of the hill, while the Omufuini's remained separate on the other. The Babukusu decided to take no part in the contest and left their cattle at home, though many of the clan came to watch.

At first light the next day they drove the beasts into rough kraals made from thorn boughs and began milking them into pots. As each pot was filled a warrior carried it up the hill to a little shelf of land at the top. The slopes fell steeply from this, bald of grass, but eased as they approached the plain, and, each party choosing a place on opposite sides of the shelf, they began to pour milk over the edge. All that morning the warriors milked, climbed the hill, and wasted the milk on the steep rock while watchers below observed how far the two streams reached. By noon, when the last drop had been wrung from every cow, the result was plain. The milk of the three clans flowed almost to the bottom before it soaked into the rock and dried, but the Omufuini's reached to the plain and vanished in the grass. Cherono had made good his boast.

He stood there with a broad smile while behind him his warriors leaped and shouted, but Nanguba and the clans that followed him were silent and would not take the discussion any further. They went home to get what they wanted done another way.

The laibon Nyang'oli told Khunya that he thought there would be trouble.

It came with the rains. War bands from the Masaba, Omwahala, and Omubichachi met secretly on the forested foothills of Masaba overlooking the Omufuini clanlands. Once they were joined, Nanguba led as chieftain. Milikwa also sent some Babukusu because he was anxious not to be left friendless if things went well, but his force was little more than a token. He had a troubled mind, could not see his way clearly, and did not want to commit himself too deeply. The Chetung'eng'i were left in ignorance.

The force slept in the forest that night, and it was a bad one, with heavy rain. Lightning struck some trees close to where the men huddled wrapped in their cowskins, backs to the rain. The wet, blasted timber smoldered and stank and many thought this a bad sign, but a soothsayer of the Omwahala said that, on the contrary, it was a good omen. In the same way as the trees had been split by a single stroke of lightning, so would they deal with the Omufuini the next day. When they heard this the warriors took heart again.

Before morning they roused and flapped the wet karosses to shake the water off the hair. The cold maize cake they carried was eaten and the hides of their shields loosened, for the rain had shrunk them and the wood frames were protesting under the strain. Then they took the skin covers off greased spear blades and left the forest in two great columns. The sun was not yet up, but it was light, the sky soft and clear, the color of a veld iris. It promised to be a fine day. Once on the plain they spread out in smaller groups and swept into the Omufuini villages, moving silently except for the whisper of skin anklets against the wet grass.

For the most part the Omufuini were taken still sleeping in their huts, and Nanguba's war band reaped lives as a man gathers thatching grass. They dragged out the women and children, who slept on the floor near the hearths. The men, who by custom made their beds high in the rafters, were for the most part left to die in the burning huts. Nothing at all was left of the villages that bordered the forest, but those deeper in the plain had time to take alarm. Here some defense was made, but by afternoon all the fighting was over. The Omufuini, retrieving what little was left them, retreated across their western border into empty land—small bands of refugees who slowly assembled under Cherono. The women wailed, and the men measured disaster's extent in silence.

The raiders did not follow, but turned back to secure what they had won. There were rich pickings of cattle and weapons, household goods, young women, and children, and encumbered with all these they returned to Nanguba's kraal to divide the spoil. The better part of the Omufuini herds had been taken; there was plenty for everyone. The women Nanguba turned over to any man who wanted them, and this greatly pleased the warriors, since most were young unmarried men with the sharp appetites of their kind and little opportunity to satisfy them. Perhaps four hundred women were judged young enough to be serviceable and these were herded together into an empty cattle kraal and told to take off their aprons. Then each warrior took out whoever pleased him, did what he wanted in the bush surrounding the kraal, and returned the girl when he had finished. This rape continued for a day and night; then the elders put a stop to it and the women were taken as wives by one man or another. A few did not survive, for they had not been used gently and a girl who caught the eye had to endure the traffic of many men. Recognized only as half-wives, for no bride wealth had been paid for them, the women were scattered across the four clans. They were merely kijiko, "things around the kitchen," as the saying goes.

"A dry thatch never burns alone." If ever a people proved the truth of that saying, it was the Bukusu. But first, let the story of the Omufuini be told to its end.

Having lost heavily of everything that makes a clan great —fighting men, women, children, and cattle—they were in a bad plight. Worse, the blow had fallen just before the new sowing, and most of what they had stored was destroyed in the villages Nanguba had burned.

When the remaining cattle were safe in rough kraals, and they had built shelters for the women and children, the men gathered, angry and despairing, and demanded opportunity to mend their fortunes by war. Cherono tried to counsel caution, but his reputation as a leader had fallen and the young men would not listen.

They waited for a full moon and then raided the Omubichachi, whose villages were nearest. Rage had not quite robbed them of all reason for they marched in a great circle around the near border and came in along the river where they hoped to be unexpected, and indeed at first they had some success and overran two riverside villages. But the kraals were empty, for the Omubichachi, anticipating something of the kind, had moved their stock onto Masaba land. Also, the men were awake and soon mustered strongly enough to drive off the attack. The Omufuini went home and on the way fell into an ambush laid for them by the Masaba. They struggled out of this with hard fighting and worse cost, and a dejected party returned to their makeshift homes, where their women wailed afresh. Cherono, trying to rally his men, gave advice which they were in no mood to accept. They bayed savagely at him in the council place and then beat him to death with their spear butts.

Fighting continued in small raids throughout the rains until harvest, and then they admitted what most of them had known for some time, that the clan lands must be abandoned and new homes found. Herding what cattle remained, they went north in a great sweep around Masaba. But the Teso, who wanted no increase of hungry mouths in a bad year, shot arrows from the forest, killing men and cattle, and the Omufuini decided there was no path in that direction. They returned, avoiding Ebukaya, where the kinsmen who had destroyed them were already spreading out into the burned villages, and trudged on southwest until they reached the river.

Here the Nzoia was fast-flowing, plunging steeply to the southern plains and eventually to the Great Lake. Making for the plains they knew only from hearsay, they decided Nzoia must be crossed. And soon, too, if they were to survive, for children and cattle were dying. They searched for a shallow ford, found one that was barely passable, and sent a few warriors across to spy out the land. The men found nothing to bother them, so the next day the crossing began. It took time since the water was deep and swift-flowing, and the cattle had to be dribbled across, and landed scattered on the farther bank. However, at last they were all across and, while some men regrouped the beasts into one herd, the rest made a living rope for the women and children.

This new country they were entering belonged to the Nandi, kinsmen to the Kamasia that Maina had fought years back, but a greater people and far more terrible in war. They did not live in villages but scattered their houses widely over the land, but this did not mean they could not act quickly enough in concert if the need arose. A man would call news of danger from his house to his neighbor on a distant ridge and the spears would soon gather.

They had seen the Omufuini some days back, the news had been tossed swiftly into the Nandi heartland, and a war band now watched the crossing from a hillside. The Omufuini scouts had missed this; perhaps, being tired, they had grown careless. The Nandi waited for the women to cross and then moved.

And so it was that the Omufuini were a mob, women

searching for children, men securing cattle, all intermingled and unprepared, when the war cry bayed and the black shields and bright spears broke from the trees. There could be no flight, for the water was at their backs; there was scarcely any fight, for the heart had left them. In an hour the men were dead and women and cattle were trudging into Nandi with new masters.

Perhaps some had remembered Maina's words as they struggled through the water: "You will go like madmen around Masaba and if you cross Nzoia River you will die."

So of the Omufuini, who had been a clan rich enough to waste milk from the top to bottom of Emabusi, nothing remained but a handful of women breeding Nandi to new husbands.

Some time later Khunya of the Chetung'eng'i, his face troubled, talked with Seriani, his war leader, and a few laibons.

His clan was small but its fighting men were hardy and practiced in arms, for they alone of the six clans had found fairly constant work for their spears during the peaceful years at Ebukaya. They held the eastern border country against the Teso, and raiding between the two peoples went on intermittently. Never serious warfare, but it was enough to keep the young men out of mischief and in constant hope of a cow or two honestly stolen.

The Chetung'eng'i, clinging to Masai customs and beliefs, had been willing to live somewhat isolated from the rest of the Bukusu so long as their fighting qualities were respected and their laibons feared. Khunya had had no fault to find with the lot of his clan in the past, but now he was far from sure. There was unrest within and the suspicion of a more serious threat than Teso raiders from without.

Ole Seriani, wizened, hard-bitten war leader, bluntly explained the former to him.

"The young men," he said, "have heard tales of Bukusu kraals bursting with Omufuini cattle, and they name your timidity as the reason a similar harvest didn't come our way. If we'd done our share in that talking at Emabusi, it might have been better. Don't misunderstand me, these aren't necessarily my own thoughts. I'm telling you what lies in the minds of those who grumble."

The laibon Nyang'oli, the same Nyang'oli who had played the fool at Emabusi, said, "It would have made little difference if we'd acted in that way, Seriani."

"No?" he replied. "It would have brought cattle. Cattle, an easy war, and perhaps a few women. They all keep young men quiet."

"Eh!" said Nyang'oli. "War, cattle, women. You can't see beyond them, like any warrior. But there's something more serious here than gaining a few cows. What occupies my mind is Nanguba. Now there's one with a real talent for greed. He's eaten a meal and the taste was good. He'll soon be looking around for another."

"That's also my thought," said Khunya, "but I hoped that he might have his eye on Milikwa's Babukusu rather than us. They'd be easier than we'd be."

"Milikwa," said Nyang'oli. "Now there's an example to us all. The dog who tried to steal two bones and lost both. Not firm enough to hold apart from Nanguba's devil's brew nor bold enough to go in deep and profit by it. So where is he now? His young men are deserting him for Nanguba, whose promises have a better smell to them, and he sits in his kraal hoping that by keeping still he'll escape notice. Milikwa grows old and his luck is leaving."

"Nevertheless," said a laibon, "his clan shouldn't be despised. If the Babukusu go down Nanguba's craw he'll be that much stronger for us to deal with. Someone should speak frankly to Milikwa and tell him he needs a friend as badly as we do."

"He won't move," said Nyang'oli, "and he won't even squawk until the knife's at his throat."

"You may be right," said Khunya, "but we'd best try him. There are certain other things that should also be done. The Bukusu are more to be feared now than the Teso. Shouldn't we look over our shoulders a little?"

"That's my work," replied Seriani. "I think the kraals should be emptied on that side. Where best can we graze the beasts; north on Masaba?"

"No," said Nyang'oli. "Nanguba used Masaba when he fell on the Omufuini. He might do so again. Nanguba's not one with a great store of ideas."

"Along the river then?"

"Yes," said Khunya, "that will be best. Is there anything else we should do?"

"I think," said Nyang'oli, "that some of the Samia might be useful if they were paid a little and frightened more. It would be good to get timely word of Nanguba's intentions. I and my brothers will do the frightening, Khunya. Would you be willing to pay?"

"I'd raise a cow or so," said Khunya, "if I thought they'd be well spent. But, Nyang'oli, you and your friends might share the cost. I've never yet heard of a poor laibon, and we all have a stake in this."

"It goes against the grain," sighed Nyang'oli, "but there's something in what you say. We'll share."

"Wah!" exclaimed Seriani. "A laibon who'll disgorge wealth with no haggling. Indeed, things must be serious!"

The Samia who crouched on the floor of Nyang'oli's house had a red slablike face. A squat man like most of his race, he was as barrel-chested as a baobab. Just now he was sweating, and in the close hut there was an acrid smell that was something more than unwashed Samia. It was, Nyang'oli concluded with satisfaction, fear. The man's name was Denge and he had been an old tenant of Maina's who now held his land from Nanguba. A brother laibon had passed him on saying that he had an interesting tale to tell. Nyang'oli, having heard it, agreed with the estimate. He took Denge through his story again.

"So Nanguba will move against the Babukusu."

"Yes," said Denge, "the Omubichachi and Omwahala with him. All three, with the next full moon."

"What about the Babukusu who've left their clan for Nanguba; will they be in this against their own people?"

"No, they won't trust them against their own blood. They're going to be used to watch you. Nanguba thinks you might cause trouble while he's out against the Babukusu. They're to share the cattle, though. There's a lot of grumbling about this."

"And how will they move? Directly along the valley or around by the mountain?"

"That I don't know for sure. I think by the mountain. They're holding a big talk in empty Omufuini country with young men from all the clans who are dissatisfied with their holdings. They say that what they're after is to share the place sensibly without fighting, but it could be part of the plan against the Babukusu. From there they'd move swiftly enough upon them across the ridges and not be seen. But I don't know."

Nyang'oli looked at his visitor thoughtfully.

"How do you know so much?" he asked.

The Samia shrugged.

"I see, I hear. If you're a Samia it pays to. Also, I have a daughter who belongs to a man called Wanyongo, and he's close to Nanguba. There wasn't any bride price; she's just kijiko. But the arrangement pays for itself in other ways."

Nyang'oli nodded. "We thank you, Denge," he said. "If you hear more we'll make it profitable for you."

It was dismissal and Denge stood and then hung there uncomfortably.

"Is there anything more?" asked Nyang'oli.

"Shall I be paid for this?"

"Didn't the laibon Sukali pay you?"

"Yes, for what I told him. I've told it again to you. I'm a poor man and I risk my throat over this."

Nyang'oli said nothing and when the Samia ventured a look at him he did not like what he saw and the sweat appeared on his face again.

"I'm sorry," he muttered. "Forget I asked. I'll go now."

"Go well," said Nyang'oli.

Outside the Samia picked up the spear he had left leaning against the wall and trudged stoically through the night to his own household beside the river. When he reached there his people were just rousing, and he called a boy who was munching cold maize cake, his eyes half closed from sleep.

"Go to Nanguba," said Denge, "and tell him that Denge says the thing's been done and they believe."

"Just that?" asked the boy.

"Yes," said Denge. "Nanguba will understand."

It took a long time to convince Milikwa of what Nanguba's real intentions were. At first the old man refused to entertain the idea, his eyes shifting uneasily from one to the other of the two laibons who were Khunya's instruments in this business. When he spoke he did so in whispers as though Nanguba, in distant Masaba, might hear him. Even when he finally forced himself to accept what they said, he refused to act in full concert with the Chetung'eng'i. He was afraid of Nanguba, but he also feared the Chetung'eng'i. He could not accept the presence of their war band inside his borders, not even to help him deal with the Bukusu when they came—if they came. He thanked them. Perhaps his own spears could deal with the trouble—if it was true there was going to be trouble. His mind heaved with fears like five-day-old carrion with maggots. The laibons tried to keep the contempt out of their voices.

In the end the best arrangement they could make was that a Chetung'eng'i force should be mustered on the forest slopes during the time of the full moon, ready to be called upon if needed.

So, at the time appointed, four hundred good warriors with Ole Seriani in command idled for two days among the trees. They slept and woke to eat their cold food sparingly, took snuff, slept again, and waited. They were still waiting when Milikwa's Babukusu, stiffened by the Omubichachi, overran them. Most of them died before they had time to lift shield or spear. Seriani rallied perhaps a hundred survivors and they went back up the mountain, fighting all the way.

By midday Seriani had found what he was looking for, a place where he and those with him could die, along with a reasonable number of Bukusu. It was the mouth of a small blind ravine and there was a trickle of water running from the rock face at its end. The enemy drew off when they saw them kraaled and so, for a time, the Chetung'eng'i could breathe and even go in small parties along the ravine to drink.

Seriani wondered whether he could get a man away with news to his clan and spoke to a senior warrior about this. The man shrugged.

"Someone *might* get past them," he said. "I don't think it likely but it could be tried if you think it worthwhile. I don't. I've seen only Babukusu and Omubichachi in front of us all day. Where are the Masaba and Omwahala? I think whoever goes will find strangers beside his hearth when he arrives. If he arrives."

"I'm inclined to agree with you," said Seriani. "Eh! That Nanguba should make fools of us I can find it in my heart to forgive. After all, there's Maina's blood in him. But Milikwa! Milikwa! I most dearly wish Milikwa were here today."

"Well, he isn't," said the man, "so you'll have to be content with those who are. Is anyone to go?"

"No," said Seriani, "it wouldn't be any use."

When it was over the Bukusu went home soberly, for

finishing Seriani had cost them a desperately high price in blood.

What was left of the Chetung'eng'i went to the mountain, as many men with pressing reasons to hide have done before and since. Their own tribe had murdered them; so few were left they could not have commanded safety from the Teso, and there were no cattle left to buy immunity. Khunya was dead, charred bones in a burned hut. Nyang'oli, the only laibon left alive, took to the mountain a handful of men and women owning nothing but the few things snatched before they fled.

Masaba draws men in their plight as the sun sucks spilled water from a broken pot. In the great forests on the deep-folded, river-bitten flanks they can find refuge forever if they wish it. To seek a man there is to look for a flea in a bed skin. An idle eye might fall on what was wanted by chance, a search never.

For days they climbed slowly among the great trees of the rain forest. Here the only paths were those traced by the windings of game, so they forced a way where it seemed no one had ever walked before. Presently the trees stood wider apart, became stunted, gnarled, and grew great shaggy beards of hanging lichen. Then they vanished, and the bamboo marched up in polished ranks and feathered plumes across buttressing hills until they in their turn gave place to heath. Here was black peat between the tussocks, strange spongy-stemmed plants the Chetung'eng'i had never seen before, and the voice of sweet cold water running everywhere. Above, the naked red rocks of the still-distant crater could be seen, but they went no farther. Here, between bamboo and heather, it was believed no one would trouble them for as long as they wished to stay. Hut poles and thatch were at hand; they stopped, built shelters, and tried to live.

But it was a fearful world they had come to. The seed they had with them would not grow, and the few goats and sheep they owned were plagued by leopards which raided fearlessly in daylight. Quite soon it was a slackly manned household which did not possess a leopard skin or two, and they were needed, for the place bred a kind of cold that bit deeper into bone than any they had known before. For days on end the clouds lay touching the earth; they were lashed with hail and icy rain, and the thunder echoed in the caves and ravines below. On days like these they shivered in their shelters and the children coughed and some died.

With time they learned that the mountain could give a living; even, occasionally, plenty. There was a root which made a flour when pounded, lily bulbs in profusion among the grasses, young bamboo shoots and fungus in the forest. And these could be found at every season of the year. The men killed eland and sometimes pig and there was a kind of great rat living among the bamboo which cooked well. When they tried again with the last of their seed the finger millet grew, stunted but heavy-eared. Arguing from custom, they had planted in the wrong season; here on the mountain the year stood on its head.

There survived all told perhaps a hundred souls; they were still the Chetung'eng'i. Living close together, they helped each other and survived. After a while, they occasionally laughed.

Marriage became a problem. Previously they had gone

outside the clan for wives, fearing confusion if they took women in their own descent. Deeply troubled, they came to Nyang'oli for advice, and the old man helped them. Part of his trade as laibon was to hold in his head how each family was related to another, and trouble had not harmed his memory. He told them that in the plight they were in now, there was no other path but for Chetung'eng'i to marry Chetung'eng'i. He searched his knowledge of the ancestors of each man and woman, drew a line across which there was to be no mingling of blood, promised to intercede with the dead for any fault done, and, to encourage them, took a new wife himself. He had lost his entire household and, knowing that his time was running out, perhaps he hoped for at least one more child to replace him. Whatever his reason, he married a girl named Mukite, and she came to him willingly enough, grateful to get such a man as this, old though he might be.

That year was one of great suffering, for it was exceptionally cold. Maina's white head was seen for months on the crater wall and even lower, where they were, snow fell. None of them had ever seen the stuff before and they wondered at the way it bit the hand when touched. As the year grew warmer they decided not to risk another season like this, and as they felt more confident now, their fear of going lower was blunted. They gathered the harvest and moved down the mountain to a string of great glades in the forest. Here they were almost as safe from discovery, there was enough grass for the animals, and the climate was milder. Some still kept their gardens in the old village above and camped there when the crop needed attention, and all the men occasionally went high to hunt eland.

In this new place Mukite gave birth to a son, which

greatly pleased Nyang'oli. He gave a feast and the people laughed with him, and it was a good thing to have happened since the next year he died.

When the old man was laid outside his house for the customary two days, everyone touched his face with pity and spoke their praises. There were no reservations in anyone's grief, for this man had served them well in adversity. Then a distant kinsman named Mufilia wa Kitalia carried the body to the hillside for the hyenas and leopards, and he said that it was no burden, for Nyang'oli weighed little more than a half-grown child. Mukite and her son went to Mufilia so that he could raise up any more children that might remain in her for his dead kinsman, and he became chief and laibon of the Chetung'eng'i.

Also that year, the young men began going down the mountain to raid and to try to even the score a little with the Bukusu.

Nanguba Masaba was a man who was never quite satisfied. When he lived under Maina's shadow it was always remarked that he ate as if his past held years of starvation and he was afraid such times might return. And this was strange, for all his life his belly had been smooth with good feeding and his hunger only in the mind. Now he ate tribes, or rather his warriors did. He himself was an indifferent performer with a spear, being gross in body and too short in the wind for campaigning. But his appetite was bottomless and remained so all his life.

He was a new kind of chief. The men who had ruled before Maina were strong men, followed by their equals when it seemed wise to do so. If the times demanded leadership, then to be strong it must be single. But when peace returned, these leaders resumed their place among the rest, except perhaps they were listened to with enhanced respect. Maina had been somewhat more than this; he was outstandingly able, but even he had considered other opinions before acting. But not Nanguba. He never listened to counsel, and no one defied him and lived. He had eaten the Omufuini, and the Chetung'eng'i were stamped out. Of the clans left, the Babukusu had disintegrated. Milikwa's young warriors had brought their spears to Nanguba and called themselves his men and of no clan; Milikwa lived privately with his eyes on the ground. Mungoma Omubichachi and Walemba Omwahala were uncomfortable in the presence of the monster they had suckled, spoke small, and avoided each other in case petty talk over a pot of beer be taken for conspiracy. But men no longer spoke of themselves as belonging to a clan. They were Bukusu and did as one man told them, Nanguba. And indeed if they were young and active it was often profitable, for war no longer happened but was sought after, and any good man with a spear could win cattle.

Nanguba sat like a gorged spider in the center of his ordered affairs and, ugly as his life might be, he was able. He left war to the men he owned, but saw to it that they were talented at the business, and from his mind alone came the way in which they were to fight. Bukusu war bands were trained in new methods, and they were like this.

Each band was divided into three parts. The first, called the Elami, were all young men armed with light spears and chosen for their ability to run swiftly and far. They scouted ahead of the main force in groups of three or four, a cloud of rapidly moving men who brought warning and information.

Behind them marched the Bayoti, "the tasters." The largest of the three groups, they were all experienced men carrying heavy, long-bladed spears and war shields of iron-hard ox hide.

Last were the Engultilti, the rear guard. Following the Bayoti, they made encirclement and surprise from behind impossible. In battle they guarded the piled war bags of the Bayoti, sitting with their backs turned to the fighting to avoid excitement or dismay, and became a reserve to be called upon if needed.

Nanguba trained his army by making them fight mock battles, in which the men were armed with sticks, until everyone knew the part he had to play. This playing at war went on in the broad valley bottom, the reeds along the river, and the forests of Masaba's foothills until the hazards of any kind of country could not break their formation either by day or by night.

When he had watched them give proof of their readiness they were sent out to raid, never more than two bands being absent at a time, one remaining to guard the homeland. The Teso, who in the absence of the Chetung'eng'i had become bold and troublesome, were the first to discover how effective these new skills were. In a place called Kiboche the plan that Nanguba had made for his warriors proved itself to be good. They crushed the Teso and afterward, under a leader named Kokanya, they swept for three days unchecked through barely defended villages gathering cattle and women as a child picks ripe berries.

Then it was the turn of several small Abaluya tribes

living south of the valley, and after them the big inland clans of the Luo from Luanda. But these heavy-limbed black men from the lake shore were more obstinate and the Bukusu took little from them. However, in five or six years a great circle of empty land was cleared round Ebukaya in which they could graze their swollen herds.

Now about this time the Bukusu were troubled by a number of raids from a people who, when they were briefly glimpsed in the light of a burning hut, seemed notably similar to the Chetung'eng'i. The damage was trifling, a hut gutted or a kraal rifled at a time, and always near the mountain. But Nanguba, thinking he had done with these people forever, was angry and puzzled as to where they came from. He sent a war band onto the mountain slopes, but although they scoured the forests for days, they found nothing. They returned eventually to report failure, which did not please Nanguba. He turned a cold eye on their leader and sent them back to search again, but with no greater success.

For some time after this he let the matter lie, but when a bolder raid touched his own herd, he sent for Kokanya, the man who had destroyed the Teso, and told him to take his full war band onto the mountain and stay there until this pest was removed. Kokanya mustered his men and searched the forested slopes from one full moon to the next, but they saw no roofs, herds, or even old turned soil, and the game they disturbed watched them fearlessly. There was no sign at all that anyone had ever lived here. The young men grew lean with sweating their way into every forest-choked ravine they found and began to mutter, while Kokanya, as hard a man as any who followed Nanguba, became anxious about the welcome that might await his return. It was not easy reporting failure to Nanguba, and at such times he had a habit of falling into fits of rage. These in themselves would have earned him no respect, but in the grip of the worst of them he wallowed on the ground, mouth wet with spittle and gross body jerking as if he danced. Obviously such visitations were sacred. Kokanya had seen it happen twice and he did not want the experience repeated or to be the cause of it, so he had the most blatantly dissatisfied men flogged and told them to search on. As an afterthought he detached a hundred of the Bayoti and sent them higher up the mountain.

"How far shall we go?" their leader asked him.

"Until you find these cursed Chetung'eng'i or vanish into the sky," he answered, which gave them little comfort.

They went up to the very edge of the crater, peered into it apprehensively, then descended by another route. It was the idle eye that discovered the Chetung'eng'i. They stumbled into the glade at evening, surrounded the huts, and killed everyone found there. When they had cooled somewhat from the first blood-spilling, they would have taken such women as still survived. But they were obstinate and ran along the glade to where a brawling river leaped into a gorge, and flung themselves onto the rocks far below. The Bukusu did not bother to go down, for there seemed no doubt that the women were dead.

They searched the huts, finding only rough hoes, poor pots, and a number of skins. Some goats were caught and quartered so that the meat could be carried. In the small fields, ripe millet was found and a number of end-of-season gourds, and they filled their empty bags with this loot. This would have been all they found if one man had not lingered for a better search of the huts; he could not believe they contained so little. In one he heard a movement above and, peering up into the gloom, he pulled a small boy down from the rafters, and was bitten for his pains. The warrior cursed, then laughed, beat the boy dazed with a flat hand, tethered him with a leather thong, and dragged him down the mountain.

A day later Kokanya brought the boy and his captor before Nanguba, who looked at him with interest.

"From what my Bayoti say," reported Kokanya, "they were Chetung'eng'i. There were only corpses to judge by, but someone had the sense to look at the women and they'd been circumcised. I don't think there are any more left. It's difficult to understand how they survived as long as they did in that place."

Nanguba looked at the boy closely. He had the redness of skin, lean face, and almost feminine lips of a Masai, but it might have been his childishness.

"Certainly he looks Chetung'eng'i," he said. "What does he say?"

"Nothing," replied Kokanya. "Hasn't spoken since we took him."

"We'll keep him," said Nanguba. "He'll make a spear when he's older. Untie him."

"At the moment he's somewhat sharp in the teeth," put in the man who had found him. "And if he's untied he'll run away."

Nanguba laughed.

"Let him run or stay as he chooses. It isn't important. As for the teeth, a dog that bites is soon cured with a stick. Let him loose."

So they untied the thong and offered the boy some

stewed meat, but he shrank away. Then he slipped under a grabbing hand and went like a squirrel across the compound, through the gate and into the sheltering bush. They laughed and went about their business, and for that day and the next Nanguba's household had brief glimpses of him watching from a distance. On the third day one of the wives found the child exhausted on the ground outside her house when she went out in the early morning. He trembled when she touched him but stayed.

She gave him water, which he drank greedily, and later milk and a little porridge. She had no children of her own yet, although she had been married for more than a year; it was a sorrow to her so she kept the boy.

Although he was long past the age when a child begins to talk, he was silent and never used a word of his own language. Gradually he understood the Lukusu that was spoken to him and in time spoke it as few men were able to do. They never learned his given name, so they called him Kisache—"he who was found." Later they added, "the Storyteller."

He was Mukite's son, the only child of Nyang'oli's body to live, and the last of the Chetung'eng'i.

Kisache

Kisache was a strange boy, and an even stranger man. Nanguba's intention for him did not come true, for he never was a warrior. When half grown, he was sick, and lay for many months unmoving on a skin in the hut of the woman who had taken him in. Although eventually the fever left him and some strength returned, the muscles of one leg remained weak and that limb was shorter than the other. So he limped, could not keep pace with other boys of his age, and eventually gave up trying to do so, making his way alone for much of the time. Since he drew no comfort and support from his age brothers, he gave love only to his foster mother, and stayed with her longer and more intimately than boys usually do even with mothers of their own blood.

Once old enough he looked after some of Nanguba's sheep and goats that grazed near the household. Later he followed the cows and here, as was to be expected, he was greatly tormented by his companions. With the cattle each child quickly learns which among his contemporaries he can hurt with impunity, and those older and stronger who do the same to him. But Kisache was a gift to all. Not even the most puny was more helpless. He was whipped with small branches, made to clench his hand on wait-a-bit thorn, forced to stand among soldier ants, and beaten with nettles—all the ways of causing pain that boys invent during the long hot idle days to serve as practice for the maturer cruelties of men. Kisache became adept at suffering, a silent, still-faced child who wept only when he was alone at night.

But being without the usual means of defending himself, he soon found different weapons. He had an eye for the oddities, weaknesses, and shames of others and within his thin body and stick arms a power of mimicry that could sketch them plain to even the most stupid who watched him. Take Bwake, hulking Bwake, whose wits were as thick as his limbs and whose greatest pleasure was beating Kisache. When Bwake ran his big buttocks shook like a woman's, and he dribbled as he spoke. Kisache showed the other boys Bwake to the life. The lean, sharp-faced Kisache miraculously became a flabby, spittle-showering Bwake, stupidity made flesh. The rest stared, recognized, and guffawed, Bwake at first among them. But when at last the oaf realized who was being ridiculed, he lumbered splutteringly to his feet to punish. The others pulled him down. They wanted to see more of this Bwake revealed, to understand how it was done. The last they never achieved, but they demanded extended performances, and, finding Bwake's attempts to end their pleasure tiresome, at last kicked him in the cods and left him howling.

There were other Bwakes and with time Kisache became accepted, welcomed, licensed, even feared.

Kisache also had another gift, one that merged with his ability at mimicry; he made stories.

"Tell a story, Kisache," the boys would say when heat, boredom, flies and the hunger ache of late afternoon became unendurable.

"About what?"

"About . . . Oh, about Uduma."

All eyes turned to Uduma, master herd bull, massive head hanging in the heat, too oppressed to graze, the wooden clapper silent on his neck.

"There isn't a story about Uduma. He's just Uduma, the red herd bull, nothing more."

"Well, tell something then. Go on, or we'll beat you."

Kisache looked closely at the bull. "On second thought there *is* something about Uduma. He's not all he seems. By day, yes, the bull you see; but at night in the darkness of the kraal he changes. Then he becomes a man, very tall, with only one eye [Uduma had been blinded by a hooking horn a year ago]; and he moves among the sleeping cows to the fence, steps over it, walks between the kraal guards, and stoops to enter the first house. . . ."

And so on.

How was it that such things fell word by word from the tongue of a cripple called Kisache? Doubtless he had heard others tell tales. The woman who fed him would have told the stories women keep for young children, and the old men by the fire at night would have provided the other, meatier sort. But the woman would tell the tales she learned as a child and the old men those of their past or of the known ancestors. The world Kisache peopled grew new within him.

Look once more at the boy Kisache.

One day he and three other herd boys, somewhat older now, swam in a dry-season pool of the Nzoia. It was afternoon, the cattle resting, no movement but the restless tails and cud-chewing jaws. Tiring at last of the silt-thick water, the boys put on their skin clouts and wandered idly down the bank to the next pool and found there three girls.

"So you've been peeping at us, have you?" said Soroti, acknowledged leader of the boys.

The girls giggled and lay about on the ground. "Peeping!" retorted the boldest of them. "What reason to peep at you? There'd be nothing to see."

"Bwake's got something worth seeing," said Kisache slyly, and Bwake smirked. The boys sat on the rocks to talk.

"Seems as if you were looking for us," said Soroti.

"No," replied the girls.

"Well, since we've met, let's play."

"We're equal numbers," said Mweya, the fourth boy.

"How equal?" asked a girl. "We're three and I see four of you."

"Kisache doesn't count," said Bwake. "He's too young and small."

The girls were willing, and they all began to discuss how they should pair off, while Kisache sat silently apart and watched. Presently, when matters seem arranged, he spoke. He began with Soroti, who had secured the oldest and most attractive girl.

"You can't play with Lontiya," he said. "Not to my mind you can't."

"Why?" demanded Soroti, staring fiercely.

"Have you considered how closely you're related? She's the daughter of Kolongolo, who's the brother of Bayemba. Now Bayemba is married to . . ." Here Kisache swiftly traced the lineage of Lontiya and Soroti and indeed, as he described it, the two were uncomfortably close in blood. "Why," he finished, "if you look at it rightly you're as good as father and daughter. Think of a father doing that with his daughter! But of course, you must act as you think best."

"But we're not father and daughter in the real sense of the words," cried Soroti.

Kisache shrugged and appeared to lose interest in any further discussion, but one of the girls now took the matter up.

"It mustn't be," she said seriously. "As he says, they can't play together, that's plain."

"Just imagine, with your own daughter," said another. "Impossible."

Soroti shook his head, baffled, and the other two boys looked doubtful.

"Well," said Mweya, "since that way won't do, let's arrange things differently. I'll have Lontiya and Kayawe can do it with Soroti."

Kisache raised his head. "But Lontiya and Kayawe, you're cousins, aren't you?" he said.

"Yes," they chorused, looking at him anxiously.

"Well, that's almost as bad. Uncle and niece together that way."

"That can't be right," said Mweya.

Kisache proved to him swiftly that it was. The girls

nodded their heads and drew away. Kisache had their earnest attention now.

"Well then," said Mweya desperately, "we'll have to change everything and start again. Bwake must give up his girl and she comes to me, while . . ."

"No," spluttered Bwake, who liked the look of the one that had fallen to him. "I want her. That's the way we arranged it and that's how it should be."

"Besides," said Kisache, "have you considered that there's also a problem here?"

There followed another rapid, fluent juggling with relationships. It turned out that Bwake and his chosen girl were to all intents brother and sister.

"Impossible," roared Soroti. "It's all words. Come on, Lontiya. Come up the river a bit and we'll do it."

There was silence from the girls. Presently one stood up and began to move away. After a moment the other two followed.

"Hey! Where arc you going?" cried Mweya.

"Nowhere." But they still moved on.

"Come back," shouted Soroti.

"We don't want to," they screeched.

"Come on. Don't go. Let's play."

They began to run. The three boys got to their feet and ran after them, but the girls only raced faster toward the village. They were going home.

The boys blamed each other furiously until they noticed Kisache was laughing.

"What's funny?" they demanded.

"What's funny," said Kisache between gasps, "is that properly considered I'm the only one here who could have

done it with any of them. I've no relations in this clan."
They beat him, of course.

As Nanguba grew older he grew crueler and more suspicious, and success gave him greater reason to be, for as the desert around the Bukusu increased there was less employment for his warriors. Nanguba would not let them marry until they had blooded their spears. If they stayed at home, idle among the kraals, they grumbled, made mischief, grew dangerous. They still held to Nanguba because so far he had brought them excitement and loot, but he was learning that to be effective, success must always be hammered bright and new. Work had to be found for the young men.

One year, after the harvest was in, he sent a war band against the Nandi, and this was his first mistake.

In the past the Bukusu had had little to do with these people, and nothing was known of their strength. They sheltered in difficult hill country beyond the river, and their habit of living scattered in small households gave the impression of a weak tribe thinly holding good land. This is, as everyone knows, a false picture, for when an enemy threatens, every Nandi knows by custom what he must do. They move with great assurance and speed, especially at night, for they do not fear darkness and reckon the owl's hoot to be a sign of good luck. In battle they are hardy and fierce, giving unquestioning obedience without bickering to those who lead. They have laibons, as the Chetung'eng'i did, men of subtle skill at interpreting the wishes of the dead and, because of this, greatly feared. Some laibons always accompany warriors in battle, where they can be distinguished by the great black-and-white cloaks of colobus-monkey fur they wear. They are unarmed except for tall ironwood staffs, and they do not fight; neither must they be harmed by a successful enemy, for that is sacrilege and eventually brings disaster. In their own wars between clans, the Nandi laibons watch closely the way the battle ebbs and flows, and if no result is likely without great damage to both, they will intervene. Then the warriors of each clan sit apart while the laibons of both confer, and what they decide is done without question.

It was against these people that a Bukusu war party, under a leader named Omumumia the Teso, tried to earn themselves a name. The Nandi allowed them to penetrate deeply into the land, and they traveled for most of a day, finding empty huts and kraals. Then, late in the afternoon, they were attacked in a steep-sided valley where the war cries of the Nandi echoed fearfully, like the screams of devils. The Bukusu broke and fled up the valley, but found it blind with tall cliffs. Having them safe, the Nandi shouted insults until night and then ran in, silently now and the more terrible for it, all softly padding feet, hissing breath, and wicked, flesh-slicing iron.

Some Bukusu got away, but not many. They climbed the creepers curtaining the cliff, hid in the forests that night, and crossed the river next day. Without shields or spears they returned to Ebukaya, hungry, beaten, and shamed. Omumumia the Teso was among them, and he would have been wiser to have died with his command. For when Nanguba heard the news he was visited by a fit of rage so violent that all who witnessed it were awed and frightened. The spirit was on him longer than usual and he crawled on the floor around the wall of the great hut, biting at straws hanging from the daub. When a man is released from the grip of such a fit he must be obeyed, and so it was here. Nanguba told his followers to beat Omumumia the Teso to death, and they did so with clubs and sticks in the compound outside the Great Hut, until it was difficult to recognize that what spread there had once been a man.

After this, many wondered what Nanguba would do next. Some privately held the opinion that it had been a mistake to destroy the Chetung'eng'i laibons, for their services and counsel were sadly needed now. However, no one thought it wise to mention this to Nanguba.

Nothing was done for a season and then Nanguba called for Kokanya and told him to gather the senior war band and lead it against the Nandi. Now the men of this band were older warriors who had been blooded in the earliest of Nanguba's wars, all married men who owned land and herds—the hard, sober, experienced fighting men of the tribe. Kokanya had a great reputation and, almost alone, courage enough to occasionally speak his mind to Nanguba.

"It would be best," he said bluntly, "if we forgot the Nandi for a time. We won't get any profit there. In my opinion what's needed is peace and a chance to forget the mess Omumumia made of things."

"Omumumia made a mess in more ways than one," said Nanguba. "Perhaps you remember that."

"I certainly haven't forgotten it," said Kokanya. "Well, you've dealt with my first suggestion, perhaps you might consider the next. The men I would have to take against the Nandi have wives, children, and kraals. The Nandi won't be easy and it's likely that a fair number of these same men will not return. Their wives will sleep cold at night and grumble. It's a strange thing, but men listen to women's grumbling. If you must send a war band against the Nandi it might lead to less trouble if you chose one made up of younger men."

"Under another war leader?" asked Nanguba. "You sound to me, Kokanya, as if you were afraid of the Nandi."

"I wouldn't say that was entirely true," said Kokanya, "not more afraid than the next man, anyway. I just want to do what seems to me best."

"Then you'd best remember what happened to Omumumia and consider how you can teach the Nandi a lesson they won't forget," said Nanguba.

Kokanya did not think there was anything else it would be sensible for him to say, so he gathered his war band (they showed little pleasure over mustering), made sacrifice, and led some six hundred men marching silently towards Nzoia. But when the river was reached, Kokanya called them together and said this.

"I don't know what's in your minds regarding this war we're sent to, but I've got some thoughts on the matter which it might interest you to hear. Are you willing to listen?"

Some spokesmen among the warriors said that indeed they wanted to hear what Kokanya had to tell them.

"Well then," said Kokanya, "hear me out. What I want to say first is that I've got little stomach for the work we're sent to do. I don't think we'll beat the Nandi, who seem somewhat formidable when it comes to war. Neither do I believe we'll get much in the way of cattle, because it appears the Nandi are well served with information about anything that's going on. I'm willing to bet that by now every cow has been moved out of our path and all that's waiting for us is a large number of unpleasantly efficient fighting men.

"Now it appears to me we can do one of three things. First, fight as we're ordered to, and I've told you what I think our chances are with that. Next, we could go across the river and poke about a bit, taking good care not to get into trouble, then come back and tell Nanguba that the Nandi were alert and had removed the cattle and it didn't seem wise to push matters further. The only thing I have against this plan is that I don't anticipate living very long after it's been carried out. Life might be made uncomfortable for some of you, also. The third possibility, in my opinion, is this. We could go down the river, skirt Nandi, and make for Maragoli. We speak the same language as those people and there's a good deal of our blood among them. We would not rush right in among the Maragoli but send a message telling them of our predicament and offering them our spears. I'd be surprised if they didn't welcome a force of our kind. We can stay there and perhaps later come back to Ebukaya. Nanguba won't live forever."

"What about our wives and children?" cried one warrior.

Kokanya looked at him speculatively and then he put down his spear and hauled up his kilt.

"I don't know what you keep under this," he said, "but you can see I've got the means of pleasing new wives and getting new children if I have to," and he grinned.

Those listening bellowed with laughter, and when they had finished rolling on the ground they agreed to follow Kokanya to Maragoli. That night a few of them had second thoughts and slipped back to Ebukaya, so Nanguba soon learned what had happened. But the rest went to Maragoli and the people there gave them land, and later women, and afterward used their spears against the Teriki.

When Kisache became a man, he took his place in the great household of Nanguba, where his ability to invent and sing a song, his wit, and story-telling were valued. It was not an easy place, for any dealings with Nanguba were as uncertain as summer milk, one moment sweet with drunken generosity and broad laughter, the next sour with evil, and no one could predict when the mood would change. Kisache walked a narrow path for, as he was a very father of mischief, often the pleasure gained from making it forced out discretion. Time and again he went too far with Nanguba. Then the hard eyes would glint savagely from their surrounding fat, the gross hands clutch dementedly at small things nearby, and Kisache had to use his wits with the agility of a flung cat to land safely. However, he was all Chetung'eng'i and, although his withered leg insisted that words must serve as spears, he preferred danger to the boredom of peace.

It was obvious to all who watched that the future held a sudden and probably violent end to their relationship, and although no one was in any doubt as to who would have the better of this, many were curious about when it would occur.

Now when news of Kokanya's desertion reached Ebukaya, there was serious discontent. The wives left behind posed a problem not easy to solve. If the men had died, then their widows would have been taken decently by near kinsmen, but what could be done about the plight they were in now? There was much debate over this, some arguing it was impossible for the women to be left and the children remaining in them not given life for the clan, and as many protesting that for brother to take a brother's wife while both men lived was confusion of blood that could only end in disaster. No satisfactory answer was found, and while the men wrestled in debate, the women (as Kokanya had predicted) found their beds cold at night. They grumbled loudly and many were prepared to listen. The year was named the Year of Half Widows and Nanguba's slaughter of the Chetung'eng'i laibons was remembered again and this time talked of more openly. Luck had left the Bukusu, men said. The ancestors were angry and there was now no one to intercede between them and the living. Lost wars and man-empty households were already here; it was all too probable that drought, famine, and disease—all the ills the dead could inflict—would follow for lack of skilled laibons. Few as yet plainly named Nanguba as the cause of this trouble but many looked in his direction and were silent.

Nanguba was neither deaf nor blind. Overbearing and occasionally possessed with madness he might be, but there was always a part of him which looked narrowly upon what was needed for his own safety. So now he took council of sorts with the elders who were still willing to speak for their clans, and among these a plan was hatched. If the Bukusu needed laibons, then the Nandi would be asked for them and paid with cattle. There was a precedent for this, for the Nandi had taken laibons from the Masai.

So three elders were chosen and they went to the Nandi

carrying bunches of flowering grass called segutiet to show they came in peace. Their plans were listened to courteously, and they were given beer and asked to sit apart while the Nandi discussed the matter. The upshot was this. The Nandi were willing to provide laibons for the Bukusu. They would begin with one and if, after a period of trial, he and his new people were satisfied with each other, more might follow. The number of cattle to be paid was discussed and, after decent haggling, settled. Secretly the Bukusu were somewhat surprised at how cheaply they came out of this, for the Nandi agreed upon a price of forty good heifers.

More beer was drunk to seal the bargain and arrangements were made final. On a named day the cattle would be driven to a place where the course of the Nzoia made a sharp elbow. Here the Bukusu would find their laibon waiting and, once the cattle were handed over, he would return with them to Ebukaya and build his kraal there. The elders returned to Nanguba well pleased with their work.

On the day appointed, forty prime heifers were driven to the Nzoia, accompanied by Nanguba, all the important men of the Bukusu, and a large crowd of the curious, eager to see what would happen on such an unusual occasion. They reached the place agreed upon, a small open water meadow surrounded on three sides by the river, with a single gray-barked morabe tree growing in the middle. There, standing in the grass, they found something bulky covered with an old, worn cowskin kaross. Nanguba took off the covering and beneath was a great, wide-meshed wicker basket of the kind men carry fowls in. It contained a young ape busy scratching fleas.

Beyond the river the hills were silent and apparently

empty, but in their minds the Bukusu were deafened with Nandi laughter. It did not seem to them that they would ever hear the end of it. They returned to Ebukaya without a great deal of talking, some boys young enough to be cheerful driving the heifers in the rear, and when he was safely home Nanguba had one of the worst of his fits. No one ever again thought it sensible to mention to him the word "laibon."

Now one night some time after this event, Kisache told a story. Nanguba was feasting in his Great Hut with a number of elders and it was an occasion when much beer was drunk. When the women had taken away what remained of the food, leaving only a few meaty bones to be toyed with and the full-bellied pots of warm beer, the serious drinking began. Kisache had a place in the outer circle of followers and Nanguba, in a better temper than he had been for some time, called for a story to occupy men's minds while they drank. At first Kisache shook his head, for usually he would only tell when the mood was on him, but Nanguba bellowed fiercely and at last Kisache came to the center of the circle and squatted, clasping his arms around his knees and staring at the ground. When the room grew still he raised his eyes and said, according to ritual, "It's in my mind and heart to tell. Will you listen?"

"Tell; we'll listen," they murmured.

"A long time ago, when the animals were more like men and women than they are today, there was a cock named Jogoo and a hare named Khunguru. They were friends, after a fashion. The hare, who was a serious-minded creature, admired Jogoo greatly—that proud strut and ringing cry, the tail that curved, flashed, and broke like falling water—although Jogoo considered Khunguru a bit of a fool. It is plain their friendship was as single-edged as an ax, as friendships often are.

"Now a day came when Khunguru visited his friend Jogoo. This was something not achieved before, and it was to be no casual encounter; he was to sleep the night there.

"He followed his host about the house, garden, and kraal all day, asking innumerable questions. He must see how everything was done, know all about this splendid friend of his. Jogoo stood it well. Arrogant he might seem to strangers, but he knew his duty as host, though long before the day was over he wished his guest at the bottom of a deep well. With concealed relief, he showed Khunguru to the place where he was to sleep and wished him good night.

"Khunguru settled himself comfortably in bed and rehearsed in his mind the day's events and all he'd learned. He was anxious that nothing should be forgotten and a full report be made to his wife at home. But as he was occupied in this way, he heard voices in the next hut. It was Jogoo and his hen retiring to bed.

"At once Khunguru was outdoors with his ear pressed to the hut wall. He listened greedily to some scraps of ordinary conversation and then he heard something that made his long soft ears twitch with interest.

" 'Wife,' said Jogoo when they were both settled upon the perch, 'tonight I find myself too tired to dispose of my head in the usual way. You must do it.'

" 'Willingly, husband,' replied the hen. 'How would you prefer it done? With a knife, or shall I just twist it off?'

" 'Better use the knife,' said her husband, 'but remember

to put the head back in the morning, won't you, in time for me to crow. I should be sorry to miss that.'

" 'Of course,' she said.

"Poor Khunguru, he was about to burst with curiosity. That his friend possessed unusual talents he knew. But this was well-nigh beyond belief! He ran silently along the wall searching for some way to see into the hut; for see he must. How else could he discover more about this wonder?

"At last he found a small hole where the plaster had crumbled and, after enlarging it gently, he put his eye there. Inside the moonlight fell upon the shapes of Jogoo and his wife upon their perch. He could see, faded and ghostly, the rainbow colors of the drooping tail and the soft breast feathers rising and falling in the quiet of sleep.

"But no head!

"It was, of course, where it always is when a cock sleeps, tucked under a wing. But how was Khunguru to know that?

"Back in bed, he wondered how such things could be. Unbelievable, but he had seen it. And it must be commonplace, for the hen had not thought it unusual. 'How should it be done?' she'd inquired, and then—wheeh! With a knife!

"One thing was certain, he must see the head replaced in the morning, even if he had to stay awake the whole night. He settled down, determined not to close an eye until dawn. And as he lay waiting, he wondered idly if he also might be capable of. . . . It had seemed simple enough . . . not even uncomfortable. . . . Why shouldn't he?

"And here, it must be said, Khunguru fell sound asleep.

"Jogoo's triumphant crowing wakened him. He struggled from sleep, cursing his failure to remain awake, flung himself to the peephole. There was his friend, arched in the supreme effort of another cry, and his head was on. Khunguru looked carefully and there was not the slightest suspicion of a seam.

" 'But of course,' he muttered. 'It's obvious, his head must be on again if he can crow.'

"He went home that morning, impressed, subdued, shaping a new ambition. He would show his friend of what he was capable. Not removing his head, of course, nothing so advanced as that. At least, not yet. Yet, why not?"

Here Nanguba interrupted the tale. This was not something he was pleased to listen to, and he said so. What had grown men to do with hares and cocks that talked? It soured his beer.

"I'm sorry," said Kisache humbly. "I fear my craft is scarcely with me tonight. Agreed, the tale is unsuitable for the company, though it's true a little more point appears at the end. However, enough. I'll stop. But I must tell you this is the last cob I have in the store tonight."

"Ah, well, we'll hear you out," said Nanguba, "but for pity's sake get quickly to this point you speak of. I'd sooner have a tale of women or war, or preferably both, than this pap of babbling animals."

So Kisache continued.

"A week later Khunguru invited Jogoo to stay with him. Jogoo was not anxious to go, but he had a strong sense of duty. He sighed and went. After all, he might enjoy himself some of the time. Khunguru was often amusing, when he didn't intend to be.

"Now it must be clearly understood that things at Khunguru's household were not so fine as at Jogoo's. He and his wife lived comfortably enough and certainly nothing would be stinted on the day he entertained his friend, but it was only ample, plain fare, and for sleeping there was no question of a separate hut for Jogoo. As is usual in all but the grandest of households, the guest had his bed at one side of the hearth and Khunguru and his wife on the other.

"Khunguru gave Jogoo time to settle on the bed skin and then embarked on his plan to impress.

" 'Wife,' he said, 'I'm too tired this night to dispose of my head in the usual way. You must cut it off.'

" 'What in the name of Khakaba are you talking about?' she said.

"Across the hearth Jogoo heard this and smiled into the darkness. So he'd guessed right when he'd thought his inquisitive friend would not be able to resist listening to anything said next door. It appeared, however, that his own wife was quicker at picking up a joke than Khunguru's. No doubt she'd had plenty of practice, living with a quick-witted husband.

"Khunguru began to lose his temper.

" 'I said cut it off,' he snapped.

" 'Oh, keep your head,' she replied.

" 'That's just what I don't want to do,' he said in a furious whisper. It upset him that Jogoo must be listening and would think that he was not master of his own household.

" 'What's got into the creature?' said his wife, and she tried a little sarcasm. 'Shall I take it off with a knife or with the ax? Just say which you'd prefer, Chieftain.'

" 'Now that's a better attitude to take,' replied her husband. 'Use which you like. Replace the head in the morning, however. I shall need it then.'

" 'Are you serious?' screeched his wife.

"Khunguru forgot himself then and bawled in a passion, 'Will you never oblige me in the slightest way without arguing? Can't you once do as you're told!'

" 'Well,' said his wife, not a particularly bright creature herself, 'if you insist. You won't like it, and neither do I. If you ask me, the whole thing is entirely unnecessary.'

"But she did as she was told, with an ax that lay handy.

" 'And untidy,' she added. 'Also it's quite obvious who'll have to clean up the mess. But then he never did consider me in the least.'

"Now Jogoo had listened to this with great interest. Toward the end of the conversation it had crossed his mind that things were being taken a shade too far, but a person of his kind does not thrust advice upon people unasked. Especially when they are in bed with their wives. So he did not interfere.

"In the morning he rose early as usual, and told Khunguru's wife that he must hurry home. The harvest called; it was in a most tricky stage. He thanked her for the hospitality.

" 'You must,' he said somewhat awkwardly, 'give my good wishes to your husband.'

" 'Yes,' she replied, a little embarrassed. 'I'm sorry he can't be here to see you off. Really, this morning he's not at all himself.'

"Jogoo, of course, did not question this and began his journey home.

" 'And properly considered,' he told himself as he strutted through the pasture, 'what she said was true.'

"And then he was shaken with laughter. 'But he as good as did it himself,' he gasped when he'd recovered a little.

'Cut it off!' he told her, and then . . . God help us, what fools some people are!' "

Kisache had done with his tale and there was a disappointed silence. Then Nanguba reached out, took a beef bone, and threw it at his storyteller.

"Out!" he growled. "Get out of my sight. I see no grain of point in anything you've said. What meaning could there be to all this?"

Kisache ducked the bone, rose hurriedly, and reached the doorway. There he paused to say, "I must ask the company to forgive me. It was indeed a poor story, for I buried the point too deeply and for this deserve your scorn."

Then he left, but outside in the darkness he must have hovered and listened for anything that might follow.

Many there stared earnestly at the ground, for they thought they had found a meaning in Kisache's story, and it was one for which they had a certain amount of sympathy.

"Well!" bellowed Nanguba, his curiosity aroused. "Is there anyone here who can explain this rubbish to me?"

Presently an old man coughed and said carefully, "It's true that this was not among the best of Kisache's stories, but perhaps what he meant to say was this. There were two creatures spoken of; one was wise and the other . . . less wise."

"That's not difficult to see," said Nanguba. "Anyone can understand that to cut off your own head is the act of a fool."

"Yes," said the old man quietly.

Nanguba's eyes narrowed.

"Ah," he said, "perhaps the word spinner was getting at

something after all. If instead of of the word 'head' we put the word 'laibon' then . . ."

He stopped to consider further.

"Yes," said the old man again, making sure that he avoided the eyes of everyone seated there.

"I see," said Nanguba, and then he roared, "Is there anyone here of like mind to Kisache?"

"That wouldn't be our place," said the old man.

"No, it wouldn't," said Nanguba trenchantly. "And neither is it the place of any crippled Chetung'eng'i get to call me fool. Mitunge!"

Mitunge, a burly thug whom Nanguba kept to carry out some of the more questionable of his wishes, slouched from where he leaned against the house wall.

"Find the cripple Kisache," he was told. "He shouldn't be far from here. Then keep him until I say what's to be done."

The man searched for Kisache, but he was not to be found. And indeed, he was never seen again in Ebukaya.

So the travels of Kisache began. He was a cripple, a man without spear, tribe, or clan, but his very helplessness preserved him from harm. Any household except that of a Masai—and they are more like vultures than men—will give porridge and a place to a stranger if he asks courteously and comes in peace. For a time. "When the visitor comes, give him food. When he has stayed a month, give him a hoe," as the saying goes, and Kisache had little use for a hoe or for any kind of work except his own. But he was welcome for his songs and, when his language was understood, for stories and wit, until idleness earned cold looks or mockery offended and the host grew blunt. Then

Kisache must move on, limping the narrow paths which, winding, dividing, and joining as they may, eventually connect everyone in Africa.

Many stories in many languages are told about Kisache. Whether they are all true, or whether some are about other strangers who stayed awhile and then left in haste, leaving angry dupes behind, it is difficult to say. One thing is common to all these tales; it seems that the man who was wronged found, when wrath cooled, enough humor in his plight to ruefully tell the tale against himself. This may be the true footprint of Kisache. There is place here for one such tale.

In Terik there lived a man named Merikwa who enjoyed the possession of a great herd. As all prudent cattle owners do in that country, he divided it in case, misfortune striking, he lost everything. Half grazed near the household under his careful eye, with a child to watch by day and drive them in at night. The rest he kept upon a good piece of land a day's march away in the care of a trusted herdsman.

Now Merikwa had two wives, both young, and properly one should have lived in each place with a good house and garden apiece, a woman with her eye on each herd. That is how it should have been by Terik notions, but Merikwa, not so young as he had been and somewhat fat and weak at the knees, had little inclination to walk for a full day whenever he fancied variety in the woman who lifted her apron for him. He was fond of that game too.

Kisache came to Merikwa in some distress, for the rains were on, the ways bad, and he was starving. The man took him in hospitably enough, gave him a bed inside the fence, and enjoyed his talk of an evening.

It happened that while Kisache stayed with Merikwa a misfortune occurred for the household. A boy arrived one night with news that the trusted herdsman had fallen sick, coughed a day or so, then died. The neighbors had buried the man and would care for the cattle (for which they would charge a heifer) until they knew Merikwa's wishes in the matter.

Now here was a predicament and the good man did not know what to do, for he loved his herd and his comfort equally and knew of no one to replace the herdsman who had died. Presently he approached Kisache and suggested he go in the man's place until someone else could be found.

"It's true you're somewhat crippled," he said, "but the work's not difficult and the cattle don't wander far there, for the grass is good. Also it seems you owe me a favor for the help I gave you and the good porridge you've eaten."

So Kisache became Merikwa's herdsman. He lived in a tumble-down shelter beneath a hill, tried to fill his stomach with little else but milk, grew even thinner than he was before, and envied Merikwa with his wives to cook for him. He had been at this troublesome business for the whole of the rains and half into the dry season when Merikwa sent word that he must drive the herd to the household. Kisache did this with the help of the boy who had brought the message, arriving at nightfall. Having seen the beasts safe in the kraal, he went to Merikwa and told him that it was done. The man was pleased.

"You can stay with me for a time as my guest," he said. "I'm thinking of marrying again and there'll be bride wealth to pay. I'll need the herd here until that's settled, so there's no hurry for you to return."

So Kisache, willingly but with some reservations about returning to that shelter under the hill, lived in a grain store within the fence and ate like a hyena everything the women cooked. It was good to experience once more the pleasure of having his guts separated from his backbone.

But, as the days passed, given to idleness and solid eating, other appetites also returned and he found his eyes following the women. One was called Bwisa and the other Mwango, both young, both personable, or so they seemed to Kisache as he watched them move about their household business, noticing the way their breasts shook as they wielded the pestle and their aprons waved as they strode in, strong-legged, bearing the water.

"One or the other, or both. Even if afterward I starve," he said and licked his dry lips, wondering how it could be done.

A morning came when Merikwa clapped Kisache on the shoulder and said, "Let's go and see the beasts. I need your judgment about those I can spare for the bride wealth." Kisache took his eye off the rounded haunch of Bwisa passing and, with an inward sigh, followed his master. They went down the hill toward the nearby herd, but when they reached the bottom, Merikwa fumbled in his kilt and clicked his tongue with annoyance.

"Tcha! My snuff. I've left it behind. Favor me and go back and get it, Kisache."

So Kisache trudged back and, as he limped, hunger honed his mind to a sharp edge.

They were picking over grain spread on a mat outside one of the houses, both bursting ripe as figs, and Kisache looked at them fondly.

"Well, Pipestem, what have you come for?" inquired Bwisa.

"To have you both," said Kisache in a dreamy voice.

"Eh! And who said you could do that?" they clucked.

"Your husband sent me back for just that purpose," said Kisache.

"Now there's one liar who can soon be proved so," said Bwisa. "By my reckoning the man shouldn't be much farther away than the castor trees at the bottom."

She walked a pace or so to the drop of the land.

"And there I see him. Call out, Pipestem, and ask if indeed we're to lie with you."

"Certainly," said Kisache, "but he won't be pleased."

"No, I don't think he will," said Bwisa.

So he stepped beside her and, cupping his hands around his mouth, he shouted, "Master Merikwa!"

"I hear," floated back a tiny voice from below.

"Your wives," cried Kisache. "They refuse to give me what you sent me back for. They won't let me have it."

"Ayee!" came a screech back. "Bwisa! Mwango!"

"Yes, man," they piped.

"Are you listening?"

"Yes, man."

"Do what he asks. Isn't it mine to give? Do it at once."

"Ayee!" they chorused in wonder.

"Did you hear me?"

"Yes, man."

And Merikwa strode away.

"Well, who's the liar?" inquired Kisache as they stared at each other in amazement.

They took him into the house and Bwisa, the elder, asked, "And which of us comes first?"

"Take your aprons off, both," said Kisache mildly, "and I'll see in which direction the inclination takes me."

"Eh!" complained Bwisa, "but it's bad when a servant gives himself airs."

"And worse when a husband lets him do it," added Mwango.

But remembering the anger in Merikwa's voice and having no wish for a beating (their husband could be a hard man), they took off the aprons and lay down.

"Oh, Mama! What a woman has to put up with in life," Bwisa said.

When it was all over Kisache put his kilt back on and limped down the hill before remembering the snuff. The exertion had driven it out of his mind. However, he put matters to rights with fair dignity and hurried below to join Merikwa with the cattle, arriving somewhat winded.

"You take a terrible time over a simple task," remarked Merikwa.

"Some might say it wasn't as simple as all that," muttered Kisache. Then he made haste to excuse himself. He must just go around the curve of the hill for a moment.

There the path began that led to Maragoli, to Nyakatch, to anywhere in the world, if you walked long enough. Kisache took it. There was nothing to go back for, since he owned only the skin covering his back.

Presently, as he limped steadily on, he whistled.

When more than half of Kisache's life was gone, either he tired of wandering, or else he no longer found it easy to discover a hearth whose owner was without a score to pay. Then he settled in distant Ukwala. The place is near the Great Lake, on the edge of Luo country. Hungry for land as the Luo are, they have always turned their noses up at Ukwala, for there the rain falls seldom and locusts breed in the dust of the plain. It was occupied thinly by small broken clans of outcasts from all tribes, men who had made incestuous marriages, warriors who had shown cowardice—human failures and dross.

Kisache came to a clan there and, asking for tenant's land, was given it. He had with him now a kind of wife, a Maragoli woman, but how these two came together is unknown; certainly no bride price was paid for her since Kisache never had it. They lived in a hut which was as pinched as their lives, all rotting thatch and crumbling walls, and the woman scratched among stones and drooping weeds in a hopeless garden while much of the time Kisache sat with hands hanging useless between his knees, thinking of how things might have been. Sometimes, when they were more desperate than usual, he worked as a laborer for richer men whose harvest was heavy and hands few; but not often, and not for long. His idleness, bitter tongue, and love of mischief soon wearied men and they cast him off.

After some years of this life in Ukwala two children lived under their roof, a boy whom they called Malo and a girl named Amolo. Malo was truly a son of the house, but Amolo was in fact not his sister. Her parents, as poor and clanless as Kisache, had died when she was a baby. Now at that time Kisache's woman had longed for a daughter, for it was a sorrow to her that after Malo no more children came, and she had persuaded her husband to let her take Amolo.

"A daughter will help us in our old age," she had said, "or bring in wealth when she marries."

It was a moment when they were somewhat more prosperous than usual, no one wanted the child, there was no hindrance to taking her. For a time she cried for a breast, but then was weaned and lived. So, because of a woman's hunger for children, Malo gained a sister and the children grew up together, with perhaps a year between them. They lived the life of the poor anywhere—that is, they played with puddles and brightly colored seeds, helped their parents when they were able to or must, and were always a little hungry.

Now when Malo was half grown, Kisache and his woman went away. Times were even more desperate than usual and Malo was told that they were going to distant Maragoli—a name, a place beyond his comprehension—to get help from his mother's kinsmen. He and his sister must watch the hut, keep the fire between the three hearthstones burning low and drive Kunzi, the one goat they owned, out to graze in the morning. And so, perhaps for Maragoli, Kisache and the woman set out in the washed gray dawn of another day and that was the last Malo saw of them.

It is good to believe that no matter what straits they are in, men will never desert their children, but it has been known to happen. Kisache was a man from whom something had been taken when a Bukusu warrior dragged him down by the leg from a hut rafter, and more lost when he lay on a sickbed and his leg withered. Also, sometimes his stories were more real to him than life, and perhaps while waking from one to the hopeless other, he was driven to try to shed something that wearied him, as a snake shuffles off an old uncomfortable skin.

Or maybe it was simpler, that they met raiding warriors or fell sick and died unremarked. Who knows?

Malo

As they had been told to do, the children drove Kunzi out among the thorns. And she, being wise and hungry and not a bit dismayed by poverty, nimbly stole a strip of green bark here and a hidden blade of grass there and made a living of it, as goats will anywhere. Amolo gathered kindling for the fire and banked the greedy flames down with earth, and at night they took Kunzi into the house with them and all three slept together on a half piece of cowhide, which was all the bedding there was.

They waited a day and another, then three, and after that the days mingled until the children did not know how many had passed. They ate what little food was in the house, stripped the meager garden, and wished that Kunzi had been in milk. Then they roamed the neighboring households and begged for food, and some fed them while others threw stones as if they had been dogs. But at last there came a day when Malo knew that the man and woman would never return and that he was all the menfolk left in that family and must look after his womenfolk. So he took up an old hunting spear of his father's, an unlovely thing with a warped black shaft far too big for him, and gave Amolo his mother's hoe to carry.

"Now," he said to his sister, "beyond what we know is the world and I'm told it's perilous big, but it seems we must go into it, for to stay here is to starve, which I, for one, don't want to do. Put this bit of hide around Kunzi's neck, Amolo, so we can lead her. I'm going to close the door to keep the snakes out of our home."

And so, leading Kunzi, they started across Ukwala plain, going east toward the rising sun.

This, of course, happened a long time ago, but the plain is not a place that would have changed greatly. The umbrella thorns are dotted across the wide folds of red soil and thin bleached grass. Their roots clamber over slabs of rock, and little heaps of empty white snail shells lie in drifts left by old floodwater. Blue-headed lizards nod in the sun and at a footfall flicker away so swiftly that it is difficult to believe they were there to be seen. And, in their season, high clouds wander above, throwing moving shadows on the earth beneath, seeming in the great empty stretch of that harsh place as small as leaves wind-driven across a lake.

But there were no clouds on the day that Malo and Amolo braved the plain, for it was deep in the dry season. The cicadas beneath the bark of small twisted trees were silent, and once the freshness of the new day had gone, it grew hot and they were hungry. Kunzi plucked at the white grass in passing and nibbled at small creeping plants still green, but for the children there was nothing to eat but a few hard wild beans and the thin seeds of grasses. And once, a few flying ants that had forgotten their time to leave the nest.

At evening they reached the banks of the Wala River, where they drank and the yellow water washed a little of the tiredness off their feet, though it did nothing for their hunger. When they wearied of watching the slow-moving current they wandered up the bank, for that way promised as much or little as the other, and the river there was too wide to cross and stank of crocodiles. It was then that Amolo began to cry, for she was frightened of spending the night in the open, and Malo frowned with worry at their plight. But presently, in the curve of one meander, they came upon a small settlement and an old woman out in the dusk penning her goats. She asked whose children they were and where they were going, and when they told her she clucked with dismay at the unkindness of the world. Then and there she milked a goat and found two cold boiled sweet potatoes for them—huge misshapen things in their purple skins, but very welcome—and she let them sleep the night in an empty granary, where the deep drift of siftings on the floor made a feast for Kunzi and soft beds for them all.

The next morning Malo gravely thanked their hostess and they walked on sturdily, following the river, until they came to a great herd of cattle grazing with three men to guard them.

Malo stared at the cows among the thorns, thick as bees. Never before had he seen so many in one place, for in the western part of the plain where they came from, the land is drier and poorer and nothing thrives but goats. He said to Amolo, "Here's wealth. The man who owns these could afford to give us food for work."

So, after shouting the customary greetings to the nearest herdsman, he said, "Tell me whose cattle you watch."

The man grinned and called to his friends below to be on their guard, for raiders were at hand, spears and all.

"I'm no raider," protested Malo. "Only a poor boy with little else in the world but my father's hunting spear. This is my sister and Kunzi is truly our goat. But I'm strong and can work. I asked who owned the cattle because it seemed to me that he must be a rich kind of man and might welcome a boy to herd his smaller beasts and a girl to carry stones from the fields."

Now at this a sourness came over the herdsman.

"If it's work you're after," he growled, "you've come to the right place. The man who owns this herd is called Gwenu and he expects little else. If it's anything pleasanter you've a mind for, go elsewhere, for he's a hard one. His tongue bites like a cattle fly, and the porridge he ladles out at the day's end is sour and thin."

"Any porridge at all would be welcome," observed Malo truthfully. "Where can I find Gwenu?"

The herdsman directed him toward a distant group of roofs, and Malo turned in that direction with Amolo and Kunzi trudging after. When they drew near they saw that this was indeed a great and wealthy household, for in the shelter of the great hedge the houses were huge and solid with clean smooth walls and roofs shining with new thatch. The children went through the narrow entrance, past the piled timbers that closed the gap at night to where, seated on a polished and beaded stool before the doorway of the finest house, sat one who could only be Gwenu.

Eh, he was fat!

His cheeks shone and the flesh beneath his chin shook with good feeding. The kaross he wore was covered with fine bull curls and swept to the ground, and he smoked a pipe with a bowl as big as a cormorant's crop. Just the appearance of him made Malo ache with hunger. All about, though at a respectful distance, wives, daughters, and servants were on the boil with busyness, and an eye over their shoulders at the mountainous man who sat there.

Amolo put her finger in her mouth and sucked it at the sight of Gwenu. But Malo first knelt, then stood up straight and greeted the great man, asked his news, and wished him health and wealth (though privately he thought that Gwenu looked in no urgent need of either).

At this Gwenu's eyes almost vanished beneath creased fat. He squinted with surprise, and dropped his pipe to the ground in a shower of sparks.

"Who are these mice, and where did they spring from?" he bellowed, and the womenfolk stopped their sweeping and pounding of grain, fluttered their hands and whispered "Who indeed?" and "Where on earth?"

Malo, inwardly a little nettled by the flurry he had caused, spoke up boldly.

"My name is Malo and this is my sister Amolo," he began. It came out somewhat louder than he had intended because of the embarrassment that visited him in such a fine and wealthy place, he being a child and a beggar to boot. But when you have cracked an egg there is no sense in leaving what is inside uneaten, and so he continued,

"I'm not large, but I'm strong and have a good hand at the management of goats. Will you let us work for porridge and a place inside your hedge?"

"Work!" bawled Gwenu. "What's that the runt says? Work? Why you're barely big enough to blow your nose, much less bell a goat."

Then he lowered his voice and glowered at Malo through the lard that wreathed his eyes.

"I know your sort," he went on, "all mouth and a stomach to match. There's enough of your kind here, Mungu knows, without adding to them."

"That's not true!" shouted Malo, for his stomach was nothing as he could very well feel, and the lie hurt him as unfairness does a child until he is old enough to know it to be a condition of life. "Not a bit true! I know I'm small, but I'm strong and have a fine hand at . . ."

"All right, all right," growled Gwenu. "I heard it the first time. Now shut up, brat, and let me consider."

Then, after a wife had retrieved his pipe and lodged its iron stem among the folds of his great mouth, he closed his eyes and sucked awhile. Presently the lids opened again, and from what Malo could see of the eyes behind, they glinted hard and shrewd.

"Now listen, Malo, or whoever it is you say you are. I'm a charitable man and I'll give you a place here. You'll herd my goats, and Mungu help you if one is lost or an unlawful plant eaten, for I'll have the skin off your back, so help me. And you'll do whatever else needs to be done. Furthermore, that giggle of a sister of yours can fetch and carry and use a hoe, if we can find one small enough for her to lift. For that I'll feed you—Asis reward my generous, foolish heart!

Not richly, mark you; there'll be no gormandizing and unhealthy gluttony, only wholesome porridge. It'll probably be the ruin of me, but I'm a charitable man. I've given my word and I'll stand by it."

So that was how they came to work for Gwenu, and work they did, for, as the herdsman had said, he was a hard man. Chief of a clan, he had married many wives and owned more than a score of servants, and the huts of his tenants stretched as far as one could see. Those who labored on Gwenu's land scarcely stopped to draw breath, for upon that stool of his, from which he rarely stirred, through eyes half closed with fat, he seemed to see everything. The most starved of his tenants' dogs never flushed a flea upon its staring ribs without he knew it, and demanded a share if he thought it worth his while.

Malo herded goats out into the cold dawn and at evening trudged home behind them in the dust thrown up by their neat, quick hoofs. Amolo carried stones from newly broken fields, beat sisal for twisting ropes, and swept the hard red earth of the compound with a fistful of ojuok twigs. Eh, but they worked! And the porridge at evening was indeed sour and thin and came but a little way up the pot. But they lived. That is almost the whole of what can be said about their years with Gwenu. Always hungry and often beaten, they grew quick noses for food and clear eyes for the behavior of men; the first because it was so hard to come by, and the second because it occurred in such rich profusion around them. In this great household there were many intrigues, and a little knowledge of them could often be turned to advantage. They grew wise beyond their years and, like the chameleon on the leaf, learned to keep still during trouble. And injustice no longer moved Malo so much as it had.

Not only did they survive, they grew and flowered, for despite everything Malo became strong and lithe and Amolo beautiful. And, being strangers, ignored and despised, they remained close, filling their emptiness with each other.

Now during these years Malo became aware of one other thing besides the clamor of his stomach and the closeness of Amolo. He discovered that in him lay the gift of kinship with animals. When he said that he possessed a fine hand at the management of goats, he spoke no more than the truth. It was something even Gwenu recognized and valued in the boy, when he noticed him at all. But during his long lonely hours as a herdboy, Malo found that it was more than goats that came trustingly to his hand.

Each day he drove the goats from their thorn-fenced pen through fields of millet and maize until, safely clear of all crops, they reached the plain. There the jostling herd slowed, spread, and searched with yellow eyes and quick lips for bark and root and leaf in the waste about them. All day they surged among the thorns, keeping just within earshot of the tocking wooden bell round the leading billy's neck, and somewhere behind them Malo slouched from one resting place in the thin shadow of a thorn to another on the sunless side of an ant heap.

Many hours he sat and often slept, for there was nothing to do but be with the flock, which looked after itself. Malo was to the goats a god to whom one turned in times of need and otherwise forgot. Reassured by his stillness, out from hiding came the small creatures of the place, the flickering ground squirrels, bushy-tailed mice, and the birds. Often, when he slept through the blanketing heat of an afternoon, he was wakened by the memory of clawed feet scrambling across his nakedness and saw the dust about him marked with small footprints. At first he was not surprised, believing they were deceived by the likeness of his still body to the brown earth. But when he spoke of it at evening to other herdboys and got back only laughter or the hard stare of unbelief, then he said no more and began to think the creatures came for another reason. Sometimes he helped himself to what the wild laid in his reach and killed with hand or stick, for the small skinned corpses impaled briefly over a fire helped to fill his hungry belly. But even then they came as if they must, and when he saw this he killed seldom, and always with a small speech to the life about him explaining his need.

There were moments of fear also, the first time when, to his hesitant whistle, an anteater dragged its leathery bulk, all ochered over with dug earth, and rooted with a dry black snout beneath his feet. The long iron talons of its bowed forelegs could have scooped the life from Malo if they had chosen to. And worse, when he woke and found curled beside him a diamond-marked snake, as thick as his leg above the knee. For one breathless minute he watched the yellow sides rise and fall, and then he ran a hand gently along its cold curves and the blunt head flickered a black tongue against his fist before sliding away in the dust. It was an age before his heart quieted, but then he was certain that he, the least of the creatures in Gwenu's household, a boy without family, clan, or tribe, had something greater than them all, kinship with a wider clan than men.

Of this, nothing was known to anyone else. Even with Amolo he flinched from explaining the thing. It was known only that Malo could handle goats and later, when he was old enough, showed the same skill with cattle. Then he was given a spear, for a herdsman must if need be show teeth against marauding leopard, lion, or raiding tribesman, and his world grew larger. Much of the year the cattle were grazed in a narrow stretch of country where the land sucked water from the river and where, at evening, they could drink. But in the depths of the long dry season the grass gave out under such a multitude of hungry beasts. Then the herd was split into smaller ones and each, guarded by a single herdsman, was driven farther afield, searching for patches of standing hay and rare, inexplicable mud wallows among the thorns of the plain. In these great yearly droughts the herdsmen walked for days, and at night, each slept among his cattle inside a rough hedge of thorns, with a spear to hand.

On such a trip as this Malo first saw the buffalo.

He had crossed the plain with thirty ribby beasts and, finding little grass, had wandered for three days until he found himself where he had never been before. Small stony hills broke the flatness here and beyond the last of these, breaking like a wave upon their southern slopes, began a forest of stunted, twisted trees. He climbed a hill to see farther, and the trees stretched to the sky, sun-whitened trunks slashed with the thin shadows of curled leaves drooping in the heat. Among them distant, bigger hills rose like islands.

At the forest edge he found grass and a water hole. The

mud of its rim had been churned by game and the ooze dotted with soiled feathers shed by drinking birds. With his simi he cut thorn branches, dragged them into a circle, and sat beside this watching the cattle, waiting for evening. As the shadows lengthened, a herd of buffalo came from the forests, five hundred or more ponderous beasts, black and solid, with heavy horns curving wickedly down. They poured from among the trees and checked at the sight of Malo, milling suspiciously, the dust of their movement settling in red clouds upon their backs. Then they accepted him and advanced again, and he heard the heavy drumming of their trot change to a squashy, sucking sound as they reached the mud. The brilliant eyes softened as black muzzles dipped to the water. They blew gently and their tangled tails fell still. They drank until Malo thought the wide pool must go dry, and he whispered to himself, "But these are the cattle of Mungu."

And later, still watching, he said, "I'll make these my own." Four days he stayed by that water hole, until the grass was gone and the cattle blared reproachfully at this leader who failed them, and each evening the buffalo came to drink. On the last night he walked among them as if in his sleep, breathing the sour leathery smell of their mud-caked hides and the hay-sweet scent of their breath, and a calf butted his knees. When they left the water he went to the forest edge with an arm flung across the back of the gigantic old bull who was their leader. Man and bull stopped when they reached the tree line, and the herd surged past them. The bull turned to peer at him through the black hair that fringed its eyes and Malo cried softly, "Go now. There'll be other meetings."

The heavy head plunged once and then the beast followed its herd, and Malo waited until the rattle of dry branches on thrusting shoulders died away.

When he returned to Gwenu's household he would have told Amolo about this, if only to get relief from the excitement that threatened to burst his heart, but the trouble he found waiting put the wonder of the thing aside.

When his cattle were safe in the kraal he searched for food. Amolo cooked for him, and not finding her in the small hut she shared with two tenant's daughters, he looked about and found her weeping in a sheltered corner outside the hedge. Questioned, she only shook her head and wept again, so he returned angry and hungry to find Gwenu bawling to all for news of Malo. He went to the great house and called that he had returned with a full tally of beasts.

"Come in," growled Gwenu and, stooping, Malo went through the doorway into the shadows of the place and stood before the man. Never before had he been inside, and the red polished floor patterned with finger whorls, the splendor of the soaring thatch, and the fine skins laid with careless richness everywhere awed him. Gwenu sat upon the protesting thongs of a stout bed with a kaross of monkey fur beneath him, scratching his stomach and considering his path.

For in the last few days Gwenu had discovered something new.

When one is as rich as he was, it is impossible to keep in mind every small detail of the great changing feast of one's possessions. It is not even desirable to do so, only necessary to make all men believe that nothing is ever lost from sight. This is done simply, by finding each day some small imperfection, a limping beast or a flawed pot, and by anger, blowing on what is only a spark until the nearest fearful servant sees it plainly as smoking ruin. No matter whose fault it be, nail it firmly to one; he will not fail to be guilty if you strike hard enough. All men have things to conceal.

Gwenu had polished this trick to perfection and so it was that Malo and Amolo, along with everyone else who worked for Gwenu, believed they were never out of his sight. In truth, he had never noticed them as anything more than a small part of the complement of cattle, goats, dogs, wives, servants, and other possessions that brought him comfort and power. Until one day he looked up drowsily and saw before him Amolo pounding grain to flour and discovered that what had been a wisp of a beggar child was now a woman and beautiful. It had happened to him before but never too often. He decided to marry her; there was always room for another wife and time for another bedfellow.

He looked morosely at the muscled youth in front of him. No one knew better than Gwenu when to be direct and when devious. Had the girl relatives or clan? It seemed not, or hardly so. Malo was all the clan she possessed and he was nothing. There was no problem.

"Malo," he began heavily, "I have it in mind to be pleased with you."

"Yes?" replied Malo warily. He had had experience of Gwenu's pleasure.

"Yes," echoed Gwenu. "It's so. In the past, of course, there have been . . . ingratitudes? Some might call them that, for I took you in and fed and sheltered you like a father. Eh, my kind heart, it's so often hurt. But there, let's not dwell on it. You're young and I forgive you."

"I couldn't help being away so long," Malo made haste to explain. "The grass is thin this year and I had to go . . ."

"Grass?" asked Gwenu suspiciously. "What has grass to do with the matter we're discussing?"

"I don't know," said Malo honestly. "In fact I don't know what we're discussing."

"Tcha! Forget the grass. I'm telling you that I'm going to honor your clan by marrying your sister."

Malo gaped. He heard Gwenu saying more but he let the sound rumble on without understanding the words. His mind ached with lacerating thoughts and in panic he tried to sort them out. There was no reason why Amolo should not join the flock of Gwenu's wives, indeed there would certainly be advantages in it for both of them, and yet—why this feeling of loss and fury? He did not know what could be done or, indeed, why anything should be done, but he knew most powerfully that first he must speak with Amolo. Now.

He forced his mind back to what Gwenu was saying.

". . . take it there's no question of blood or kinship which should stand in the way of the marriage, eh?"

Malo stared at him.

"Well, is there?" blared Gwenu.

"No. Nothing," said Malo.

"Then there's only the matter of bride price to be discussed with you. Now, let it be said plainly, Malo, you're both of my household and owe me everything. Everything, I say, and so in simple truth there's no real call for bride wealth, since what's mine is in a sense yours and what's yours is mine. It's somewhat foolish to pay oneself, and that's what I would be doing if you take a proper view of the matter. However, old customs must be kept. I want no trouble in the future and, as everyone knows, I'm a just man. That's often been the cause of sorrow and loss to me, but, eh! One must live with one's nature."

He paused, breathed deeply, and then shot at Malo, "You can take five goats from my flock. How about that, eh? Could anything be more generous?"

Malo said nothing. Again he was not listening.

Gwenu twisted his blubbery mouth, closed his eyes, and opened them again. In one so puny he had not expected to find such bargaining skill.

". . . and a heifer," he drew up from the depths. "And you can choose every beast yourself. Now consider that."

He actually squeezed out a tear, which ran down the vast curving slope of one cheek and hung among the bristles of his chin. He stirred and wiped it away.

"Ah, when I think of all . . . perhaps, on further consideration, I had better do the choosing. I've greater experience in these matters and . . ."

Malo said, "Amolo isn't my sister."

". . . unbelievable as it may seem to you, one can't always leave these things to . . . What's that you said?"

"Amolo's not my sister."

"But you call her . . ."

"No matter what I call her. She was brought up in our house but she's not of my blood, and that being so . . ."

Gwenu took a breath that seemed it might empty the house of air, and he swelled.

"Then why do we sit here babbling of bride wealth?" He beat his fists upon the bed until it creaked. "Lies! I'm encompassed by creatures whose whole lives are a dung heap of lies! Why, Snake's Egg, must I speak of my marriage with you? Tell me that!"

"Because you won't take Amolo," shouted Malo. "You won't marry her!"

The man on the bed became very still, only a vein pulsing in the monstrous throat, but when Malo looked back from the doorway he saw the face squirm. He became beside himself with hatred.

"No!" Malo screamed. "I'll marry her myself!"

Then he was out in the dusk and the hanging smoke of cooking fires, and his mind began to work. Ignoring the roars of rage erupting inside the house, he went swiftly in search of Amolo. She was where he had left her, but dry-eyed now at the sound of Gwenu's choking bellows. He held her hard by both arms and demanded angrily, "Do you want to marry Gwenu?"

She shook her head and by the misery and fear on her face he knew that indeed this was true.

"Then waste no time. Gather what you can and be outside the hedge by the goat hole as soon after dark as you're able to. Is that understood?"

Again she nodded and looked so desperate that Malo's heart turned over with love and pity.

"Don't be afraid," he said more gently. "We can live without Gwenu's porridge."

Then he slipped through the shadows to the granary where he slept. He took a worn skin cloak, his herd spear, and the old hunting spear of his father's to which long ago he had added a new shaft. Outside, the bustle of men searching began, but it was dark now and he felt no fear, only a cold fierceness. He took bearings on the noises around him and then went through the alleys and byways of the household like a breath of wind, snatching a knife in one house, a bag of grain in another. When a man passed, he hung motionless in the shadow of low-jutting eaves with his knife up, then as footsteps retreated ran quickly over bare, swept earth to the overhang of the enormous hedge. When he reached the gate there were three men blocking it, so he shrank away and recrossed the compound. Turning a hut curve too quickly, he ran into a cluster of silent women huddled fearfully round a fire. They screamed in chorus, but by the time men came panting questions, he was gone through a weakness in the hedge known since childhood, running freely down the hillside with the shouts growing thin behind him.

He made for the small watercourse where the women drew their water, his cautious toes recognizing damp gravel, the shards of a broken pot. All about him was the shrilling of mosquitoes. Only a thread of water ran now between the rocks, and upstream in a clump of cane he cached his hoard of stolen goods and waited until the cicadas were silent and the real night began. Then he left everything except the two spears and crept back up the hill.

The goat hole where he had told Amolo to meet him was behind the great house, a small tunnel through the tough, close-growing ojuok stems, just big enough for a dog or a goat. It had been cut once and kept open by constant passage of animals as the ring keeps open the hole bored in the lobe of an ear.

Amolo was not waiting and, after a little thought, he lay down at the tunnel entrance and wriggled cautiously through. There was nothing notable to be seen except, to his right, the glow of a dying fire. For a moment he considered this but, finding no harm, pushed out and stood up, waiting for his eyes to become accustomed to the deeper darkness inside the hedge.

To his left, Gwenu said, "Our goatherd's returned for his bride."

His voice was rich with satisfaction and the man he spoke to, pressed against the hedge on Malo's other side, snickered his appreciation.

Malo could see plainly now. The woman lying on the ground beyond the fire was certainly Amolo. She neither spoke nor moved, so it seemed that she was either dead or bound. It was all very plain; they had watched and taken her at the goat hole. Then they had waited on the chance he would come looking for her.

"Don't hurt him now more than you can help," continued Gwenu in a reasonable voice. "We can teach him gratitude better by daylight."

And then the man against the hedge came grabbing.

Malo's fear and despair boiled over in rage. He flung the hunting spear with all his strength at Gwenu and heard that lion scream shrilly. Then he turned with the war spear on the jackal. The thought went through Malo's mind that they had not expected him to be armed, since the man only carried a club. Then the leaf-shaped blade of hammered iron sliced through muscle and tendon, jarred against bone, and the hedge broke under the body falling into it.

He ran to the girl on the ground and Gwenu, wallowing

between them with the hunting spear through the fat of his leg, switched from screams to babbling cries for mercy and flailed his arms on the earth. Malo ignored him and bent over Amolo, saw her eyes move bright with terror as he stooped. When he cut the sisal rope that tied her, she flinched and exclaimed softly at the black blood smearing the blade.

"Up," he urged fiercely and drove her toward the goat hole. She hobbled with the stiffness that came from ropes and ill-treatment, but he saw her vanish purposefully, and he gathered the bundle of small possessions they had surprised her with, and followed. Beside Gwenu, he paused.

". . . anything," gabbled Gwenu, clutching at Malo's feet. "Cattle, wives, land . . . anything, so long as . . ."

The promises tumbled over one another like grain running down the side of a maize heap.

"Just my spear, Lard-pot," said Malo grimly, and the man flailed like a cow in a mud wallow as the weapon was levered out.

Beside the hedge he gave a last look around. The fire glowed quietly, the great house shouldered its bulk into the starlit sky, and behind it men's voices were stirring. He considered the fire and then grinned evilly.

"Let's give them something to occupy their leisure," he murmured. He returned swiftly to the fire, plucked out a brand, and blowing on it as he moved, ran to the house. Reaching above his head, he thrust deep into the thatch. Then he ran.

Over his shoulder he saw fire run up the roof like a small, quick animal, pause, and lick as if in doubt. Then, parched with years of sun, the mountain of thatch exploded and a great hand of flame clawed its way up into the night. He heard shouts and a wail of women before he dived for the goat hole and a world where things might be different.

That night they moved across the plain to the river and hid in a bed of reeds that choked one of its deep curves. In this sea of tall, flowering grasses, they rested all day. Amolo slept as though she would never wake; Malo roused often to squirm on his belly to the edge of the reeds where he could see open country. Toward afternoon he watched five of Gwenu's herdsmen, armed with spears, pass purposefully. They did not bother about the reeds, and Malo eyed them as they followed the line of riverside trees until they were out of sight. He thought they might do something about him and Amolo if they chanced upon them, but otherwise he did not believe they would search overhard. By most of those he employed Gwenu was not loved. To fall in with a party of the man's grown sons, relatives, and clan dependents would be a different matter; these men had hopes for the future and favors to ask.

At evening he roused Amolo and they mixed a little raw flour into a paste with river water and ate. Poor stuff, but they dared not light a fire and anyway had no pot to cook in.

"Where are we going?" asked Amolo.

"To the country of the cattle of Mungu."

"And where's that?"

"You'll see," said Malo with his mouth full of gritty dough. "Just follow me in this, for I know where we'll be safe."

After this she asked no more questions about their future and they set out by starlight.

At noon three days later they stood upon a slope of one of the bald, sun-washed hills and stared across the shaggy pelt of the forest below. It was, if they had known, the old forest of Wala, which had, ages ago, before the Witch of the Lake robbed the land of most of its rain, marched clear across the plain to the Nandi Hills and merged there with the taller trees of the rain forest. But with the coming of drought the lowland trees had retreated, making a last stand here where the hills captured a little moisture from the lake and skies. The roots of ancient olives and figs went down unbelievably deep to water which hid in the bones of the land, and such wild animals as remained found shade and a thin covering of the grass they needed for life.

"That's where the cattle of Mungu live," explained Malo, pointing south, and although Amolo did not like the unwelcoming look of the place and was afraid of the beasts they might find there, she took comfort from Malo's confidence and trusted him. And so they made their way into the forest.

It was a poor word for this place, for there was nothing sappy or soft in it. Beneath the tortured white tree trunks there was some speckled shade, but the red pinnacles of termite heaps reached up between the branches and on the floor the creatures had covered each dead twig with a dry crust of earth. The only living things they saw were droves of small tortoises going their snail way across the shimmering sand of an open glade. Everywhere was silent and empty, for in the sun-smitten afternoon all things hide to keep alive.

They trudged all day toward the greatest of the distant

hills, reached it at evening, and slept with their backs against a rock face that held the day's heat for half the night. Thirst made it impossible to eat, but on going around the hill's shoulder next morning they found, running from a narrow, high-walled cleft, a quick-flowing stream of bright water. They stared, exclaimed, then dropped their bundles to fling themselves down, laughing, and drink. Finally they tore off hot clothing and soaked gratefully in the kindness of that joyful water.

Presently Malo sat up and looked at Amolo with the water making beads upon the bloom of her brown skin and said, half to himself, "You're beautiful, Amolo. Why have I never seen that before?"

She looked at her hands, and her smile quivered before it vanished. Suddenly he remembered how she had looked the first time they had met Gwenu, how she had stared and sucked a finger, and he rolled with helpless laughter at the thought. At this Amolo looked indignant, then grave, and got to her feet to dress again in her apron.

The stream ran free for only a hundred paces before it slowed, spread, and vanished into the sand, and where this happened there was a wide patch of brilliant green with the white heads of marsh flowers nodding over it. They became curious as to where the water came from, so they followed it up the cleft. This was narrow and strewn with fallen rocks but after winding once to the right, it opened and there they found something that made them pause and stare. It was a small, gently sloping valley firmly held between great cliffs, while above, all around, the bulk of the hill rose to a distant, jagged skyline. At the valley's end, down a precipice of red stone, the stream fell in a thin feather of spray. Ferns and creepers hung in the mist at the cliff's base and then the water was swallowed in a tangle of canes and reeds over which large flies hawked on brilliant wings. The stream ran from the reeds down the middle of the valley, dividing its floor into two long meadows. There were a dozen great fig trees scattered haphazardly, one crawling creeper-like up a cliff face, its branches rooted again in cracks of the rock. Except for the small talk of water, there was silence.

They gazed upon all this wealth with deep satisfaction.

"Here we'll live," said Malo, and Amolo nodded and began to gather the makings of a fire.

They built a house hard against a cliff face beneath the largest of the fig trees, and they did it with a decent respect for custom. When he had chosen the site, Malo drove a peg where the center post would stand, tied to this a strip of hide, and with his knife looped in the free end, drew on the ground the plan of its walls. Along this circle he dug holes, each a pace apart, and then he took his simi to the forest and cut wall posts to fill them. He cut more poles for the conical shield of the roof and pile upon pile of thinner, more flexible lathes to weave together the framework of both walls and roof. All these he dragged back to the valley and left scattered in the grass near where they would build. Then he spent one whole day searching for a center post that matched the vision he had of it in his mind. He found it at last, a straight tough stem of wild olive twice the height of a man and ending in a cupped fork. He dragged this home also, its butt leaving a lizard's-tail mark in the dust behind, and dug a hole for it with his simi where the center peg had stood. That evening, they solemnly placed in the hole a little grain and a pinch of ash, and each spat into it a mouthful of water. Then they bedded the post there, making it firm.

Neither was Amolo idle. With Malo's knife she cut reeds, tied them in shocks, and piled these beneath the cliff overhang. Fifty or more loaded journeys she must have made from the reed bed before she was satisfied, for thatching a house uses an unbelievably large store of reeds. Also, she tore bark strips from the poles Malo brought and threshed them into cords to tie the timbers.

When all these preparations had been made Malo said, "Tomorrow we build."

Amolo nodded and then asked in an anxious voice, "Have the neighbors been invited to help?"

Malo shook his head sorrowfully and said, "They were asked, but one and all begged us to excuse them. Some tale of a building of their own in hand. It would be courteous to believe them. I'm afraid we must do it all ourselves."

Amolo wrung her hands and clicked her tongue with dismay, then laughed and said briskly, "And that doesn't displease me either."

A new house must be begun and finished between dawn and dusk of a single day if there is to be any luck in it, and so they began work when there was only a hint of cold light in the valley. Also there is a man's part and a woman's part to building, and if the walls and roof are to contain happiness and fortune, these must be kept apart without confusion. So at first Amolo had to sit idle and watch Malo settle the wall posts and wrench and weave and bind and trim. But as soon as this framework of the walls was complete, she was up and carrying mud from the stream on a slab of bark and plastering the wattle with her hands. While Malo hung like a spider on the roof as it grew into a stout web that creaked beneath his weight, the walls crept up, red and solid and whorled all over with the print of Amolo's hands.

They worked all that day without food or rest and despaired of finishing in time. Hardest was Amolo's waiting while Malo thatched. She could only watch and throw up the bundles of reeds as they were called for, while she itched to climb there herself and spread and layer faster. This, however, could not be, for with a woman on the roof those standing below might see her naked thighs and this would bring scandal. Although here there was no one to see such a thing, she thought it best to hold to custom in case there was more to it than she knew.

But as the valley darkened it was done. With the sweat growing cold on them, they stood back for a moment gazing on what they had made, frowning at a ridge of thatch lying ruggedly or a rib showing through the daub, but not inclined to damn the whole for small imperfections.

"Come, let's take our things inside," said Malo.

"Patience," replied Amolo. "There's one more thing to be done for my house."

Then she went to the stream and brought the three flat stones marked days before and arranged them where, unfailingly, the hearth must stand. This done to her satisfaction, she called him within and so, invited, he came. And that also was as it should be, for the house is the wife's; the husband's life belongs to the world outside.

That night, contained by walls and thatch, Amolo waited

with bent head for Malo to untie the strings that fastened her apron, for this first time a woman must play a reluctance so complete that if her husband did not help her to overcome it she would sit all night clothed beside the bed skin.

There seemed to be no end to the business that filled their days. Digging sticks had to be whittled from ironwood, a garden broken on both banks of the stream, water carried to it, and a sowing made from the maize, millet, and beans stolen during that night's hurried rifling of Gwenu's possessions. There was little seed left, for they had had to eat, but if all went well they thought it enough to get a first crop. Frugally husbanded, this would leave sufficient for a bigger sowing in the next rains. Beneath the reeds at the end of the valley, Amolo found clay, and with it coiled a pot, smoothing it lovingly and etching patterns on its curved belly with the teeth of a wooden comb. She fired it in a blaze of small thorn branches, where in the heat it shattered and Malo rolled on the floor helpless with laughter at the disenchantment on her face. Then she spat out the single word, "Husbands!" and went back for more clay with her head held high. This time it worked, for with the new clay she mixed grit from the ground shards of the spoiled pot, and so the first trial was not wasted.

While they waited for a crop they lived somehow. In the swamp outside the valley there were lily bulbs, bitter and crisp, and after rare showers they gathered flying ants. Malo scoured the forest for ostrich eggs, but never solved the problem of carrying more than three or four safely home when he found them. He made a bow and blunt bird arrows to kill the sleek, inquisitive hyrax that peopled the ledges of the cliffs. And one day, when all else failed and the pot had been empty for too long, he took a knife and was absent all day. He returned at evening with a buck, a slender-necked gerenuk, across his shoulders. Amolo marveled that he had done this with only a knife but when he lowered the body and began to skin and joint it, he would only say, "I sat and called and it came. I begged forgiveness and explained our need before I killed, and I don't believe the ghost will trouble us."

She laughed at him. Even later while she cooked the stew she continued to be shaken by giggles at the memory of what he had said. And he had said it and remained serious and not laughed with her!

Before they ate, he took a slab of meat and dropped it in the flames to spit and shrivel there. She asked him peevishly if good food was got to be wasted, and he replied seriously, "The spirits of every place must have some share of what's taken from them."

Amolo kept silent and made no further protest. It was true enough, of course, though she had never noticed him to be over-scrupulous in this way before.

It was during one of these recurring searches for food that he saw the buffalo again. It was noon, and they were settled to endure the worst hours of the day, the whole herd standing patiently chewing or lying in thin shade, immense black heads hung down in sleep. There was no sound from them, only occasionally a flank twitched to unsettle a biting fly or a tufted tail flourished. He stood for some time believing himself unseen. Then he noticed, a hundred paces to the right and wrapped in an invisible cloak of cunningly chosen shade, a young bull watching him with massively leveled head, and beyond the herd another sentry bull. He approved of this; they were no fools, his friends. Even in this empty wilderness they watched and trusted nothing.

The sentry bull snorted and pawed the stand, but Malo ignored him, for among the huddle of bulky bodies he had seen the old patriarch who led, and he went to greet him. As he advanced, every head lifted and all movement died until the great bull came grunting to its feet, glaring with cold distrust. Then it made a snoring noise of pleasure and lumbered forward to meet him, to blow upon his outstretched hands and permit the wet black muzzle to be caressed.

After this they met some four or five times, for the buffalo stayed in the area, though they never rested in the same place twice. One evening he came upon them grazing and walked with the slowly voyaging herd, picking ticks from leathery flanks and listening to the tearing sounds of wrenched grass stems. He walked until it was dark and the beasts more sensed than seen or heard as they drifted like ghosts about him. On that occasion he came home in the first hint of dawn to find a sleepless Amolo anxiously waiting. All he would reply to her reproachful questions was, "I've been with the cattle of Mungu," and his eyes shone feverishly with the memory of it. She did not know whether to spit at him or laugh, and this too joined the list of things concerning Malo that she did not rightly understand.

And then one night while he was drifting into sleep he heard, outside the valley but close, the indignant bleat of a calf. He sat up and shook Amolo awake.

"Come," he said. "I'll show you the cattle of Mungu."

He pulled her, still sleepy, to her feet and led her outside the hut. The valley was soft with moonlight and they went along the stream to the black mouth of the cleft and all he would answer to Amolo's questioning was, "Wait, and you'll see."

Beyond the cleft the moon bathed sand and cliffs and twisted scrub in a cold clear light. Beside the swamp, against the deep slate-blue of a tree, a tribe of deeper shadows moved and broke like a wave. A hoof splashed and sucked as it was withdrawn from mud and there came over Amolo an unbearable sense of being watched. She would have fled back to the hut, but Malo held her and said she must be still. Then he whistled high and clear like a shrike and the shadows rolled forward, becoming sharp-edged until they stood all around, a monstrous thicket of beasts. The light touched curved horns and brute shoulders, sparkled on eyes and wet muzzles. They were engulfed by buffalo, pressed close, deep-breathing, and Amolo knelt in the sand, clutched Malo's knees and hid her face against him, until he turned her head and whispered, "Look, and don't be afraid. We're safer with them than we've ever been in our whole lives."

After this, Malo's strangeness became quite clear to Amolo; her man was a magician. There was nothing in this to strive to cure or to fear, so long as the power was honored and respected by both of them.

So life was peaceful for these two. The tiny crop came up and flourished in the sheltered watered valley. First came the beans, and when they hardened and dried in their shriveled pods, the millet ears turned from green to gold and at last black. Malo shaped a wooden pestle and, when they had carefully stored away next season's seed in a cobbled skin bag, Amolo pounded grain on a cup-shaped rock they had found beneath the waterfall and at last they ate porridge again. Last of all, the maize put out its tassels and the cobs grew fat in the green wrapping of their shucks. The plants stood high, higher than they had ever seen corn before, towering above Amolo's head as she walked among them testing the plumpness of the cobs. Their valley was a very fertile place that had, it seemed, waited since the beginning of time to be tilled.

They were content. In their contentment they played together with words sometimes, as few men and their women do. Malo would wait for the evening meal to be prepared and sing the old song of children at a feast.

> My belly is hanging loose.
> What are you going to put in it,
> Oh, you old woman?
> My belly is hanging loose,
> What are you going to put in it?

"Patience," Amolo would answer, busy with the pot and the stirring ladle, and then turn his words against him, singing,

> My belly is hanging loose.
> What are you going to put in it,
> Oh, you old man?

"Now, that's not at all the kind of thing which should be said by a modest housewife," protested Malo.

"Neither am I an old woman," returned Amolo.

They were content. It is true that sometimes a worm

nibbled at the perfect leaf of Amolo's happiness so that she looked uneasily at Malo and wondered how, at one and the same time, he could be the familiar one who sat outside a hut and whittled a pestle, yet also the stranger who walked in the night with the beasts and was neither gored nor trampled.

Once, unexpectedly, she asked, "Malo, will you leave me for the beasts?"

He looked up with surprise.

"Why should I go from where I want to be?" he asked in return.

"I don't know; but then I didn't know I'd married a magician. What shall we do here, Malo?"

"What do you mean, what shall we do here?"

"Here, alone, lost from men."

"How are we alone when we have each other? Foolishness! And there'll be others, more Malos and Amolos who will find us and be grateful to stay. Also you'll have children; we'll begin a tribe. When the children come I'll take each one of them and show them to the cattle of Mungu, and they'll know then that the child is one of us and can never harm them or be harmed."

He forgot her and dreamed aloud.

"The tribe will be called the People of Malo and we'll be part of this land. That is the name we'll go by with other tribes, but to ourselves we'll be the People of the Buffalo, Those of the cattle of Mungu. Only that last name must be too sacred even to be used among us. We'll know it, be taught it when we come to manhood, and it will stay in our hearts but never touch our lips. Only I, perhaps, who fathered the tribe and am brother to the beasts, might use the name, I and those who follow in my place. . . ."

And he babbled on of their future.

"Yes," said Amolo with a sigh of pleasure, "there'll be children."

And indeed a little later she knew that she was going to have a child.

The rains came and with the first drenching shower the bare and dusty scrub became green almost overnight. The sand erupted into a carpet of gaily colored flowers, flaming fiercely in what little time they had, and Malo went in search of wild-gourd seeds.

It was strange that they had never seen any growing near the valley, for the country was right for them. Gourds were needed to store their grain, to carry water on hunting trips, for ladles, bowls, and a dozen other purposes. Malo went out in the early morning determined that no matter how far he had to search he would find them. The fruit would be hard-ripe and ready for use and there had not yet been enough rain to rot them; they would plant the seed inside and never want for the things again.

He wandered most of the day and at last found them. When, at late evening, he came to the valley entrance there were half a dozen hard globes slung by their trailing, withered vines over his shoulder, and a store of ripe seeds bagged in a square of hide tucked into the waist of his kilt. He ran between the cliffs with the gourds clashing, anxious to show his finds to Amolo, but at the inner opening he checked like a squirrel in mid-flight and stared. Where the hut had stood was a circle of broken, split walls and across it the charred, still-smoking beams of the roof. A great petal-shaped stain of scorching wavered up the rock face beyond.

He made a mewing sound in his throat, the gourds cascaded onto the ground, and he ran like a madman to the ruins, pulling aside the blackened beams and burning his hands. He found nothing of what he feared and then, a little sense returning, fell back and began to look about.

Away from the hut a skin bag of grain lay split and rifled. He smelled it and knew it had not been touched by fire. Strewn around were more of their possessions—a broken pot, a bird arrow, a piece of hide. He turned to the standing corn and saw where it had been trampled and some of the stems broken when the green cobs had been twisted off. He straightened up from studying them, gripped his spear, and looked carefully up and down the valley. Shadows were creeping across it now, for the sun was below the hill, but it appeared to be empty.

He turned back to the ruined hut and a gleam of color in the grass caught his eye. He reached down and found the tiny cupped leather stopper of a snuff gourd, decorated with black-and-red beads. He knew it at once, for he had often seen it in the hand of Gwenu's chief herdsman, a bowlegged man with jutting teeth. Half the man's head was a glistening scar on which no hair grew, for he had fallen into the fire as a child. He was a relative of Gwenu's and trusted by him.

Malo ran out of the valley to cast around the foot of the hill in a great circle. There was barely light enough to see when he found what he was searching for—the tracks of men crossing a stretch of sand, many of them, he thought at least ten. The marks were more than half a day old, for the edges had crumbled and an ant lion had dug its crater of shifting sand within one heelprint. Among them he found marks of Amolo's smaller feet.

He stared despairingly in the direction they pointed. It was almost dark, the raiding party would have gone far, and what could be done supposing he did catch up to them? He returned, drank at the stream, and ate a little of the spilled grain. After this he crouched with his back against the cliff face, close to where the hut had stood. Sleepless in the dark, his thoughts struggled like a hornet in a web, and whenever the smoldering pile that had been a house settled and flared afresh into small fires they lit answering fires in his brooding eyes. Toward morning he knew what he would try to do, and when this was settled his body slid down and he curled and slept.

In the morning he made a meal of green cobs. Then he took the torn bag, cobbled together its rents, and filled it with all the grain he could find. With this and his spear, knife, and simi, he left the valley. He followed the tracks and hung on them until he was sure he had not been mistaken; they led north without faltering. So he abandoned them and turned in another direction. For the whole day he searched the forest, at times climbing trees in order to enlarge his view, but it was not until early evening that, bowed with weariness and worry, he found the buffalo. They were at rest beside the same water hole where he had first seen them. He went to drink and bathe in the thick, stinking water of the wallow, emerging almost as mud-smeared as the beasts. Then he propped his back against a tree and watched them. They were growing restless; their time of cud chewing was almost over and he knew that soon they would begin to graze, cropping grass far into the night.

He studied the plain northward with a herdsman's eye. The rains, if as yet one could give them that name, had endured some twenty days now and there had been showers most evenings. One fell while he sat, chewing millet beneath his tree; a warning spatter of heavy drops followed by a brief drenching downpour that washed the mud from his shoulders. There had been enough rain this year to spring the new grass, and although, seen close up, it grew thinly, from a distance it painted the gentle folds of open ground with green. For this he was thankful. Without the grass he did not think what he planned could be done.

Presently the old bull stood up and walked a few paces, lifting its head so that the gaunt throat stretched in deep cords of muscle. It bellowed hoarsely, clapped its fringed ears, dropped muzzle to ground, and began to graze. The others struggled heavily to their feet and, after a few protests and some confusion among the calves, lumbered forward searching for grass.

Malo rose with them.

"Now, cattle of Mungu," he said softly, "let's see how you answer to the herdsman."

It took three days to cross the plain and for Malo they were a year, a lifetime, an age. The buffalo moved only for one narrow purpose, to graze and drink, and the very plenitude of grass was an enemy to Malo's purpose, for where it grew they stayed until it was cropped too short to be grasped by their snatching black, rubbery lips. Where, for some reason, it grew more thinly, they would move decisively, but not necessarily in the direction he wanted. He tried herding them but soon learned that this was impossible. They were too big a herd for one man to dominate and, unlike cows, they had no fear of him. When he slapped their flanks and shouted they lifted heads and stared, then thrust him aside good-naturedly. He found that the key to what control he had lay in the patriarch bull; where he led the rest would follow. So Malo ignored the herd and plunged into a battle of will, understanding, and love with this immensely experienced and wise brute. He also could not be driven, but he could be called. If Malo went ahead and whistled he would come, usually, in time.

Eh, but it was slow, for the lives of these creatures followed an unchanging custom commanded by their appetites. In the morning they grazed and moved; in the brazen heat of the day they ruminated and slept wherever shade was to be found; at evening they found water and drank until their flanks swelled and the water spilled from their throats. At night they moved and fed until the small hours then milled together and settled to sleep with only the sentry bulls upon their feet. The first show of dawn found them wandering and again grazing. Grass and shade, grass, water, and sleep, and grass again. These were the fences of their nature, outside which Malo could not move them. With the consent of the old bull, he struggled to keep them a weapon in his hand.

It was fortunate that he knew the country and every water hole in it, for without this knowledge he would have failed. As it was, in all that weary snail's journey there was only once that Malo really despaired.

The plain had an arid heart, a desert core where there was nothing but bald caked earth scattered with slabs of loose pumice and clumps of aloes. They reached the edge of this on the morning of the second day and the bull stopped, lowered his nose, and blew through dilated nostrils upon the iron earth. Then he lifted his head and glared across the red desolation stretching before them. For the first time he would not come to Malo's whistle. He would not go either, but hung there, torn between instinct of what his people needed for life and this uncomfortable love of the power within Malo. He bellowed with pain when the man called, but would not come. Malo flung his arms about the harsh neck, scratched the mud-caked dewlaps, soothed and wept and implored. The bull trembled and shook its troubled head, then finally bellowed again and moved forward. Malo ran ahead whistling, but the beast had made up his mind and needed no further encouragement. The walk quickened to a trot and the herd followed. For the next hour Malo was hard pressed to stay with them, for they broke into a lumbering run and kept it up across the empty miles until grass again showed ahead. Then they stampeded, the slam and beat of their hoofs rolling across hard ground until the noise softened on soil and they slowed, panting, their mouths trailing threads of foam. They lowered heads and grazed. Malo, empty and weak, caught and passed them again, and lay flat upon his face until his heart quieted. Then, dry-mouthed, he again forced himself to lead.

They reached the long gentle slope that led to Gwenu's household deep in the night of the third day, and the herd slept huddled in the open as they preferred to at night. Malo did not sleep but sat with his back against the old bull and shivered a little, for there was a raw dampness to the night. He had reached such a state of hunger and exhaustion that he scarcely knew himself as Malo; he had been with the beasts for so long that he almost thought himself one of them. The humanity had dropped from him piece by piece during the journey and now the whole of life seemed bent to the scent of grass and water, the salty smell of sunburned earth. It was the dead time of night and, where before he would have sworn that nothing stirred and no sound lived, now he heard the termites eating beneath the soil, a rock shrinking in the cold, a sisal leaf unfolding from the hard spike of its center. And, above all, the slow-beating hearts of the cattle sleeping around him.

When the herd sensed the new day, they woke and stood to graze, and Malo led them up the slope and into the fields. They spread in a great crescent, eating contentedly, and he heard the splashing noise of trampled corn and the crisp bite and wet chewing of sap-filled stalks and leaves. Gently he inched them toward the great hedge and now their heads began to lift and they stirred uneasily at the smell of houses, dead fires, and the reek of men.

It was gray light when the first of the household came yawning through the gateway with the smoke from cooking fires beginning to rise behind them. There were four, all men, and they stopped and gaped at the buffalo, black and enormous in the dawn with the ruined crops all around them. It was the moment, Malo knew, when all his slaving could have been wasted like spilled water in sand, when beasts and men could have fled from each other, leaving him nothing. Indeed, with cries of alarm, three of the men turned to run, but the fourth was hardier. He yelled in fury at the waste of corn and then flung his spear straight at the old bull. In spite of haste and anger it was a good throw, for it gashed a heavy shoulder, then, glancing, cut the haunch of a cow standing near. Blood ran suddenly and Malo saw the bull rear and scream with pain and fury. Then, head down, with powerfully twisting haunches, it charged, and like a moving mountain the herd followed.

They went through the hedge like a rock tumbling through grass and into the houses beyond. There, hemmed in narrow alleyways, stung by the embers of trampled fires, confused by cries from the huts and by bitter, unaccustomed scents, the buffalo went berserk. With flattened ears and wild staring eyes, they charged everything that moved.

Malo followed, appalled, dodging for his life from house to house, calling desperately for Amolo. He saw men gored and tossed and trampled, a hut lean and fall with a crash, and a buried beast come screaming in fear and fury through a rain of falling beams and thatch. He saw flame leap from the eaves of a hut and blossom in a great bursting flower on the grass roof. He saw Gwenu's beaded stool kicked bounding across a swept mud floor, saw the soft, shaking bulk of Gwenu go groveling on hands and knees along a torn hedge, and heard the wail of women flighting through the gardens beyond.

In a house still standing he found a trembling Amolo and took her hand and drew her to the doorway. Most of the cattle of Mungu had gone now; they could be heard lowing in the distance and their place had been taken by a chaos of flame and acrid, rolling smoke. He led her through the tattered hedge and down the hill. They ran bent, close to the ground, like quail, but they need not have troubled, for no one was concerned with them. At the foot of the hill the buffalo were still milling, cows crying for calves separated in the riot, but they were calmer now and able to recognize their friends. Malo walked through the herd fearlessly and Amolo followed.

There was a shout from above and when they looked it was Gwenu, holding a torn skin over his gross nakedness, and behind him a huddled rout of men and women. He stared down at those two walking among the buffalo and then held up one hand in the gesture of warding off evil. Ignoring him, they began their journey back. Once they stopped at the sight of cattle and goats wandering untended, and Malo, choosing carefully, cut out a young bull, several heifers, and a number of goats.

"He promised me something for a bride price," he said. "All men should be helped to pay their debts."

Herding these, they went on with no fear of pursuit. Behind them the buffalo plodded, anxious to put distance between themselves and the memories of their own rage, but soon they drifted away on a course of their own, forgetting all in the scent of new grass.

This happened a great time ago and Malo's people, the People of the Buffalo, have long since gone from Ukwala. The place is empty and dry and the forest has shrunk, but it is beyond dispute that once they were here, for everywhere you find the round dished stones on which they ground their grain. And if you stand on the highest of the bald hills you can see below circles marked in a lighter color than the reds, duns, and olives of the plain. This is where the houses stood; the mark stays long after the walls have fallen and washed away and the thatch rotted and been carried off by ants. It is something to do with the soot of fires and the custom of people going around and about; it stains like berry juice and never quite washes out.

It seems that his people were numerous once.

From the same hill you can just see the distant lake and

a snake's track where once the river ran, and far away in one place it is as if someone had laid a deep-furred kaross over the land. That is all that remains of the old forest of Wala. It contains something increasingly rare today, or at least it did until a few years back: buffalo. There were just three of them, huge and black with cold suspicious eyes, coming and going like ghosts among the gray trees. If they have not gone yet they will soon, for all three were bulls; the nearest of their kind are two hundred miles away, and between is Gwenu with his roads, railways, towns, and his endless, greedy search for profit.

GLOSSARY

Geographical

Masaba	The Bukusu name for Mount Elgon, a 14,000-foot mountain on the border between Kenya and Uganda.
The Great Lake	Lake Victoria, the great East African lake whose shores are shared by modern Kenya, Tanzania, and Uganda.
The Great Valley	The Rift Valley in Kenya.

Religious

gods	The two most commonly invoked gods of the Bukusu were Wele Nyasaye and Khakaba. Both were usually malevolent and anyone encountering them by accident would die. Wele was also mainly responsible for sickness and the death of children, and rather obscurely connected with water. Both could some-

times be placated by sacrifice, and white hens were kept in a special house for this purpose. Only one man in each clan was permitted to sacrifice to Wele.

Mungu is a general Swahili term for God and is common throughout East Africa.

African oaths are, like ours, either sexual or religious, and I have used all three god names as expletives.

ancestors — Most African peoples have a religious attitude toward their ancestors. A clan is a continuum of the dead, the living, and the unborn. Thus land vacated by the living is still possessed by the dead buried there and therefore by the clan. Hence also the importance of a woman's being given the opportunity of bearing all the children of which she is capable; the existence of a widowed or unattached woman is a crime against the clan, since it murders unborn members. There was no such thing as a spinster or neglected widow in pre-modern African society.

Social

tribe — An African tribe may consist of several million people or only a few hundred. Its members may possess a common culture and language, but this is by no means always so. A tribe can only be defined as a group of people who, for historical and geographical reasons, think of themselves, or are regarded by others, as united. It approximates far more closely what we would call a nation than did the American Indian tribes, which in Africa would in many ways resemble clans.

clan — This is a group of people who believe themselves to have descended from the same ancestor, either mythical or real. All members of a clan speak the same language and share one culture. Some small tribes are, in fact, clans, but this is unusual. Most tribes of any size contain a number of clans. The Bukusu, as described in this book, are fairly typical of a medium-sized tribe. They are shown as made up of six clans, three Bukusu and three "out-clans" of, respectively, Masai, Teso, and mixed descent. The Masai and Teso clans would retain their own customs and probably their languages. At times there would be bitter warfare between clans.

Marriage within the clan is usually regarded as incestuous, unthinkable. Since clans are frequently too large for all members to know one another, the first thing an African boy asks when he meets a strange girl of his own tribe is, "What is your clan?" Her answer determines the relationship which is possible between them.

language — Most languages of European origin build by altering the ends of words (suffixes); African languages usually alter the beginnings of words (prefixes). Thus we would use the form *Pole* for a single man, *Poles* for the people, *Polish* for the language, *Poland* for the country. An African would use *Mkusu* for one man, *Bukusu* for the tribe, *Ukusu* for the country, and *Lukusu* for the language.

circumcision — For men this was the same operation as in other cultures; for women, excision of the clitoris. The custom had a significance which went beyond hygiene; it was carried out in late adolescence and marked full acceptance as a mature member of the clan or tribe.

clothing — A man would wear a single animal skin, either knotted over one shoulder or wrapped around his middle, whichever was most convenient for his occupation at the moment. I have referred to this as a kilt. A woman wore only a brief, rectangular piece of leather covering the pudendum; this I have called an apron. Children would be naked; small girls might wear a string of leather or beads around the loins.

kaross — A large skin of any fur or hide used as a cloak or sleeping blanket, usually worn only by an elder or other man of importance. The Nandi were noted for the beauty of their kaross, which were made from a number of pelts of long-haired, black-and-white colobus monkeys.

kraal — A cattle enclosure. I have used the southern African word as being better known; in Kenya it would be "boma." In tribes such as the Nandi, or the Bukusu of this time, which were culturally based on the possession of cattle, the kraal was the center of a large household and the word was extended to mean the entire household.

household — An important Bukusu household would contain a man, his wives and children, and a number of relatives, retainers, and their families. Each wife would have a separate house and garden and the husband would be fed by and sleep with them in rotation.

marriage — Bride wealth, or a bride price, was paid by a man or his family to the woman's family upon marriage. This should not be regarded as the purchase of a woman; it had important social implications. The bride wealth had to be repaid either in part or whole if the marriage broke down, and both families would make every effort to avoid the loss and social upheaval which would result from this.

The levirate is practiced by most East African tribes; a widow goes as wife to a brother or near kinsman of the dead man so that she may bear children for the clan.

kijiko — A Swahili word meaning literally "a thing around the kitchen," euphemistically, a concubine.

laibons — These were a professional class of witch doctors, wizards, wise men, and medical practitioners. Originally Masai, they were imported by the Nandi and other tribes.

weapons — The main weapon of the East African warrior was a heavy stabbing spear. The blade shape of these varied greatly among the tribes, and a man could identify a tribe by the shape of a spear. Bukusu and Nandi blades were leaf-shaped, while those of the Masai were narrow, up to three feet in length, and fishtailed, with a central strengthening ridge. They were made from cold-hammered iron, and many tribes protected them from the weather with skin gloves soaked in grease. Leaving these wrappings in place was often the only indication given that an armed war party came in peace. Light throwing spears were used for hunting and carried by herdboys. Bows were also children's weapons; the arrowheads varied from pointed metal or wooden barbs to blunt wooden plugs used for knocking down birds.

simi — A warrior might also carry a simi, a double-edged, leaf-shaped sword without hilt or pommel. The blade broadened and was therefore heavier toward the point end. It was used as both a tool and a weapon.

About the author

HUMPHREY HARMAN first went to Africa from his native England during World War II and, after the war, returned to become a teacher in Kenya. Now he lives in Zambia, where he trains teachers at Chalimbana College.

He learned the stories of the Bukusu from his students of many tribes over a period of several years. "I made them write and talk about their peoples as part of their work," he recalls. "I stayed at their homes during holidays, small thatched huts set among untidy fields, and met their people, usually simple peasants whose sons and daughters were the first generation to learn to write and read. My interest in their stories intrigued them, and they would go to great pains to see that I got something right, often calling in old men and women because it was known that such-and-such man 'had the best version.' I wrote down what I heard, and when I had an immense collection of stories, something interesting began to emerge. My informants spoke not only of their own people but also of their neighbors, and often the tales married. I had history of sorts."

All the material Mr. Harman had gathered coalesced for him during several weekends he spent on Mount Elgon, the Masaba of this book. "There among the bamboo and elephant, beneath the crater wall white with rime in the early morning, all that I had heard about Masaba came alive."

Mr. Harman is the author of two previous books about Africa, *Tales Told near a Crocodile* and *African Samson.*